The

Time Keeper

The

TIME KEEPER

—— ○ ——

Mitch Albom

ⒽⓎⓅⒺⓇⒾⓄⓃ
New York

THE END OF THE WORLD
Words by Sylvia Dee
Music by Arthur Kent
Copyright © 1962 (Renewed) by Music Sales Corporation (ASCAP)
International Copyright Secured. U.S. and Canada rights owned
by Music Sales Corporation and other international rights owned by
Music Sales Corporation and Edward Proffitt Music. All Rights
Reserved. Used by Permission.

Library of Congress Cataloging-in-Publication Data

Albom, Mitch
   The time keeper / Mitch Albom.—1st ed.
     p. cm.
   ISBN 978-1-4013-2278-6
 1. Time—Fiction.   I. Title.
   PS3601.L335T57 2012
   813'.6—dc23
       2012019424

Hyperion books are available for special promotions and premiums.
For details contact the HarperCollins Special Markets Department
in the New York office at 212-207-7528, fax 212-207-7222, or email
spsales@harpercollins.com.

Book design by Betty Lew

FIRST EDITION

10 9 8 7 6 5 4 3 2 1

SUSTAINABLE FORESTRY INITIATIVE
Certified Fiber Sourcing
www.sfiprogram.org

THIS LABEL APPLIES TO TEXT STOCK

This book, about time, is dedicated to Janine, who makes every minute of life worthwhile.

The

Time Keeper

PROLOGUE

A man sits alone in a cave.

His hair is long. His beard reaches his knees. He holds his chin in the cup of his hands.

He closes his eyes.

He is listening to something. Voices. Endless voices. They rise from a pool in the corner of the cave.

They are the voices of people on Earth.

They want one thing only.

Time.

Sarah Lemon is one of those voices.

A teenager in our day, she sprawls on a bed and studies a photo on her cell phone: a good-looking boy with coffee-colored hair.

Tonight she will see him. Tonight at eight-thirty. She recites it excitedly—*Eight-thirty, eight-thirty!*—and she wonders what to wear. The black jeans? The sleeveless top? No. She hates her arms. Not the sleeveless.

"I need more *time*," she says.

Victor Delamonte is one of those voices.

A wealthy man in his mid-eighties, he sits in a doctor's office. His wife sits beside him. White paper covers an exam table.

The doctor speaks softly. "There's not much we can do," he says. Months of treatment have not worked. The tumors. The kidneys.

Victor's wife tries to speak, but the words catch. As if sharing the same larynx, Victor clears his throat.

"What Grace wants to ask is . . . how much *time* do I have left?"

His words—and Sarah's words—drift up to the faraway cave, and the lonesome, bearded man sitting inside it. This man is Father Time.

You might think him a myth, a cartoon from a New Year's card—ancient, haggard, clutching an hourglass, older than anyone on the planet.

But Father Time is real. And, in truth, he cannot age. Beneath the unruly beard and cascading hair—signs of life, not death—his body is lean, his skin unwrinkled, immune to the very thing he lords over.

Once, before he angered God, he was just another man, fated to die when his days were done.

Now he has a different fate: Banished to this cave, he must listen to the world's every plea—for more minutes, more hours, more years, *more time.*

He has been here an eternity. He has given up hope. But a clock ticks for all of us, silently, somewhere. And one is ticking even for him.

Soon Father Time will be free.

To return to Earth.

And finish what he started.

BEGINNING

$$\ast\; 2\; \ast$$

This is a story about the meaning of time

and it begins long ago, at the dawn of man's history, with a barefoot boy running up a hillside. Ahead of him is a barefoot girl. He is trying to catch her. This is often the way it is between girls and boys.

For these two, it is the way it will always be.

The boy's name is Dor. The girl is Alli.

At this age, they are nearly the same size, with high-pitched voices and thick, dark hair, their faces splashed with mud.

As Alli runs, she looks back at Dor and grins. What she feels are the first stirrings of love. She scoops a small rock and tosses it high in his direction.

"Dor!" she yells.

Dor, as he runs, is counting his breaths.

He is the first person on Earth to attempt this—counting, making numbers. He began by matching one finger to another, giving each pairing a sound and a value. Soon he was counting anything he could.

Dor is gentle, an obedient child, but his mind goes deeper than those around him. He is different.

And on this early page of man's story, one different child can change the world.

Which is why God is watching him.

"Dor!" Alli yells.

He looks up and smiles—he always smiles at Alli—and the stone falls at his feet. He cocks his head and forms a thought.

"Throw another!"

Alli throws it high. Dor counts his fingers, a sound for one, a sound for two—

"Ahrrgunph!"

He is tackled from behind by a third child, Nim, a boy much larger and stronger. Nim crows as he puts a knee in Dor's back.

"I am king!"

All three children laugh.

They resume their running.

Try to imagine a life without timekeeping.

You probably can't. You know the month, the year, the day of the week. There is a clock on your wall or the dashboard of your car. You have a schedule, a calendar, a time for dinner or a movie.

Yet all around you, timekeeping is ignored. Birds are not late. A dog does not check its watch. Deer do not fret over passing birthdays.

Man alone measures time.

Man alone chimes the hour.

And, because of this, man alone suffers a paralyzing fear that no other creature endures.

A fear of time running out.

Sarah Lemon fears time is running out.

She steps from the shower and calculates. Twenty minutes to blow-dry her hair, half hour for makeup, half hour to dress, fifteen minutes to get there. *Eight-thirty, eight-thirty!*

The bedroom door opens. Her mother, Lorraine.

"Honey?"

"Knock, Mom!"

"OK. Knock-knock."

Lorraine eyes the bed. She sees options laid out: two pairs of jeans, three T-shirts, a white sweater.

"Where are you going?"

"Nowhere."

"Are you meeting someone?"

"No."

"You look good in the white—"

"Mom!"

Lorraine sighs. She lifts a wet towel from the floor and leaves.

Sarah returns to the mirror. She thinks about the boy. She pinches the fat around her waist. Ugh.

Eight-thirty, eight-thirty!

She is definitely not wearing the white.

Victor Delamonte fears time is running out.

He and Grace step from the elevator into their penthouse. "Give me your coat," Grace says. She hangs it in the closet.

It is quiet. Victor uses a cane to move down the hallway, past the large oil painting by a French master. His abdomen is throbbing. He should take a pill. He enters his study, filled with books and plaques and a huge mahogany desk.

Victor thinks about the doctor. *There's not much we can do.* What does that mean? Months? Weeks? Is this the end of him? This can't be the end of him.

He hears Grace's heels pacing on the tile floor. He hears her dial the phone. "Ruth, it's me," she says. Ruth, her sister.

Grace lowers her voice. "We just came from the doctor . . ."

Alone in his chair, Victor does the math of his dwindling life. He feels a breath shoot from his chest, as if someone choked it out. His face contorts. His eyes moisten.

As children grow, they gravitate to their fates.

So did Dor, Nim, and Alli, the three children on that hillside.

Nim became tall and broad-shouldered.

He carried mud bricks for his father, a builder. He liked that he was stronger than other boys. Power became Nim's fascination.

Alli grew more beautiful

and her mother warned her to keep her dark hair braided and her eyes lowered, lest her fairness encourage the bad desires of men. Humility became Alli's cocoon.

Dor?

Well. Dor became a measurer of things. He marked stones, he notched sticks, he laid out twigs, pebbles, anything he could count. He often fell into a dreamy state, thinking about numbers, and his older brothers left him behind when they went hunting.

Instead, Dor ran up the hills with Alli, and his mind raced ahead of him, beckoning him to follow.

And then, one hot morning, a strange thing happened.

Dor, now a teen by our years, sat in the dirt and wedged a stick in the ground. The sun was strong and he noticed the stick's shadow.

He placed a stone at the shadow's tip. He sang to himself. He thought about Alli. They had been friends since they were children, but now he was taller and she was *softer* and he felt a weakness when her lowered eyes lifted up to meet his. He felt as if he were being tipped over.

A fly buzzed past, interrupting his daydream. "Ahhhh," he said, swatting it away. When he glanced back at the stick, its shadow no longer reached the stone.

Dor waited, but the shadow grew even smaller, because the sun was moving up in the sky. He decided to leave everything in place and return tomorrow. And tomorrow, when the sun cast a shadow exactly to the stone, that moment would be . . . *the same moment as today.*

In fact, he reasoned, wouldn't every day contain one such moment? When the shadow, stick, and stone aligned?

He would call it Alli's moment, and he would think of her each day at that juncture.

He tapped his forehead, proud of himself.

And thus did man begin to mark time.

The fly returned.

Dor swatted it again. Only this time it stretched into a long, black strip, which opened into a pocket of darkness.

Out stepped an old man in a draped white robe.

Dor's eyes widened in fear. He tried to run, to scream, but nothing in his body responded.

The old man held a staff of golden wood. He poked Dor's sun stick and it rose from the dirt and turned into a string of wasps. The wasps created a new line of darkness, which opened like a pulled curtain.

The old man stepped through it.

And he was gone.

Dor ran away.

He never told anyone about that visit.
Not even Alli.
Not until the end.

Sarah finds time in a drawer.

She opens it looking for her black jeans and instead discovers, buried near the back, her first watch—a purple Swatch model with a plastic band. Her parents gave it to her for her twelfth birthday.

Two months later, they divorced.

"Sarah!" her mother yells from downstairs.

"*What?*" she yells back.

After the split, Sarah stayed with Lorraine, who would blame Tom, her absent ex, for every wrong thing in their lives. Sarah would nod sympathetically. But each of them, in a way, was still waiting on the man; Lorraine to admit he was wrong, Sarah to have him rescue her. Neither thing happened.

"*What*, Mom?" Sarah yells again.

"Do you need the car?"

"I don't need the car."

"*What?*"

"I don't need the car!"

"Where are you going?"

"Nowhere!"

Sarah checks the purple watch, which still runs: it is 6:59 P.M.

Eight-thirty, eight-thirty!

She closes the drawer and yells, "Focus!"

Where are her black jeans?

Victor finds time in a drawer.

He takes out his calendar book. He sees the next day's itinerary, which includes a 10 A.M. board meeting, a 2 P.M. conference call with analysts, and an 8 P.M. dinner with a Brazilian CEO whose company Victor is buying. The way he feels, he'll be lucky to get through one of those.

He swallows a pill. He hears a buzzer. Who is coming at this hour? He hears Grace walking down the hall. He sees their wedding picture on his desk, the two of them so young, so healthy, no tumors, no failing kidneys.

"Victor?"

She is at the study door with a man from a service company, who pushes a large electric wheelchair.

"What's this?" Victor says.

Grace forces a smile. "We decided, remember?"

"I don't need it yet."

"Victor."

"I don't *need* it!"

Grace looks to the ceiling.

"Just leave it," she tells the service man.

"In the hallway," Victor instructs.

"In the hallway," Grace repeats.

She follows the man out.

Victor closes the calendar and rubs his abdomen. He thinks about what the doctor said.

There's not much we can do.

He has to do *something*.

Dor and Alli were married.

They stood at an altar on a warm autumn night. Gifts were exchanged. Alli wore a veil. Dor poured perfume over her head and declared, "She is my wife. I will fill her lap with silver and gold." This was how it was done in their day.

Dor felt a warm, calming feeling when he said those words—*She is my wife*—because ever since they were children she was like the sky to him, forever around. Only Alli could distract him from his counting. Only Alli could bring him water from the great river and sit beside him and hum a sweet melody, and he would sip from the cup and not even realize how long he had been staring.

Now they were married. It made him happy. That night he observed a quarter moon through the clouds, and he used it to mark the moment, the light of the night they were wed.

Dor and Alli had three children.

A son, then a daughter, then another daughter. They lived with Dor's family in his father's house, near three other houses made of wattle and daub. Families lived together in their time—parents, children, and grandchildren—all under one roof. Only if a son acquired wealth would he move to a house of his own.

Dor would never acquire wealth.

He would never fill Alli's lap with silver and gold. All the goats, sheep, and oxen belonged to his brothers or his father, who often swatted Dor for wasting his time with silly measures. His mother cried when she saw him hunched over his work. She felt the gods had left him feeble.

"Why could you not be more like Nim?" she asked.

Nim had become a powerful king.

He had great riches and many slaves. He'd begun construction of a massive tower, and on certain mornings, Dor and Alli would walk past it with their children.

"Did you really play with him when you were a boy?" his son asked.

Dor nodded. Alli took her husband's arm. "Your father was a faster runner and a better climber."

Dor smiled. "Your mother was faster than us all."

The children laughed and pulled at her legs. "If your father says it, it must be true," she said.

Dor counted the slaves working on Nim's tower, counted them until he ran out of numbers. He thought about how differently his life and Nim's life had turned out.

Later that day, Dor carved notches on a clay tablet to mark the sun's path across the sky. When the children reached to play with his tools, Alli gently moved their hands away and kissed their fingers.

History does not show it,

but as Dor grew older, he dabbled in every form of time measurement that science would later credit to others.

Long before the Egyptian obelisks, Dor was catching shadows. Long before the Greek clepsydras, Dor was measuring water.

He would invent the first sundial. He would create the first clock, even the first calendar.

"Ahead of his time." That's a phrase we use.

Dor was ahead of everyone.

Consider the word "time."

We use so *many* phrases with it. Pass time. Waste time. Kill time. Lose time.

In good time. About time. Take your time. Save time.

A long time. Right on time. Out of time. Mind the time. Be on time. Spare time. Keep time. Stall for time.

There are as many expressions with "time" as there are minutes in a day.

But once, there was no word for it at all. Because no one was counting.

Then Dor began.

And everything changed.

One day, when his children were old enough to run hillsides on their own, Dor had a visit from King Nim, his childhood friend.

"What is this?" Nim asked.

He was holding a bowl. There was a small hole near the bottom.

"A measure," Dor answered.

"No, Dor." Nim laughed. "It is a useless bowl. Look at this hole. Any water you pour in will drip out."

Dor did not challenge him. How could he? While Dor spent his days with bones and sticks, Nim led attacks on neighboring villages, took people's possessions, declared that they must follow him.

This visit was unusual, the first in many moons. Nim wore an impressive wool robe, dyed purple, a color of wealth.

"You know of the tower we build?" Nim asked.

"It is unlike anything I have ever seen," Dor said.

"That is just the start, friend. It will take us to the heavens."

"Why?"

"To defeat the gods."

"Defeat them?"

"Yes."

"And then?"

Nim puffed out his chest. "Then I shall rule from above."

Dor looked away.

"Join me," Nim said.

"Me?"

"You are clever, I know from our days as children. You are not mad as the others say. Your knowledge and these . . . things . . ."

He pointed to the instruments.

"They could make my tower stronger, yes?"

Dor shrugged.

"Show me how they work."

For the rest of the afternoon, Dor explained his ideas.

He showed Nim how the shadow from the sun stick lined up with his markings, and how pointers on the stick broke the day into parts. He laid out his collection of stones that charted the stages of the moon.

Nim did not understand most of what Dor said. He shook his head and insisted the sun god and the moon god were in constant battle; that accounted for their rise and fall. Power was what mattered. And power was what awaited him once the tower was complete.

Dor listened, but he could not see Nim storming the clouds. What chance would he have?

When their conversation finished, Nim grabbed one of the sun sticks.

"I will take this with me," he said.

"Wait—"

Nim pulled it to his chest. "Make another. Bring it when you come to help with the tower."

Dor looked down. "I cannot help you."

Nim ground his jaw back and forth.

"Why not?"

"I have my work."

Nim laughed. "Putting holes in bowls?"

"It is more than that."

"I will not ask again."

Dor said nothing.

"As you wish." Nim exhaled. He stepped to the doorway. "But you must leave the city."

"Leave?"

"Yes."

"Where?"

"That does not concern me." Nim examined the carvings on the sun stick. "But go far. If you do not, my men will force you onto the tower—as they will the others."

He moved past the bowls and lifted the one with the small hole in it, turned it over, then shook his head.

"I will never forget our childhood," Nim said. "But we will not see each other again."

Sarah Lemon is running out of time.

It is 7:25 P.M. and her black jeans—which she finally found in the washing machine—are now tumbling in the dryer, on the highest heat, and her hair is so unruly she wants to cut it off. Her mother has twice returned to her room, the last time holding a glass of wine, and offered an opinion on Sarah's makeup. ("OK, Mom, I got it," she said, dismissing her.) She has chosen a raspberry T-shirt, the black jeans—*if they ever dry!*—and the black boots with the heels. Heels will make her look thinner.

She is to meet her boy outside a convenience store—*Eight-thirty, eight-thirty!*—and maybe they will eat something or go somewhere. Whatever he wants. Until now, they have only seen each other on Saturday mornings at a shelter where they work. But Sarah hinted several times about getting together and last week he finally said, "Yeah, OK, maybe Friday."

Now it is Friday and she feels goose bumps on her skin. A boy like this—popular, good-looking—has never paid attention to Sarah before. When she is with him, she wants the minutes to go slower, yet until she sees him, they cannot pass quickly enough.

She looks in the mirror.

"Ahgg, this hair!"

Victor Delamonte is running out of time.

It is 7:25 P.M. The East Coast offices will be closed but the West Coast will not.

He picks up the phone. He dials a different time zone. He asks for Research. While he waits, he eyes the books on his shelves and does a mental inventory. *Read it. Never read it. Never read it . . .*

If he used every minute the doctor said he had left, he still wouldn't finish all these volumes. And this is one room. In one house. Unacceptable. He is rich. He must do something.

"Research," a female voice says.

"Yeah, it's Victor."

"Mr. Delamonte?" She sounds nervous. "How can I help?"

He thinks about Grace and the wheelchair she ordered. He will not give up so easily.

"I want you to get on something right away. Send me whatever you find."

"Certainly." The researcher taps her keys. "What's the topic?"

"Immortality."

❧ 9 ❧

That night, after Nim's visit, Dor and Alli climbed a hillside to watch the sun set.

They did this almost every evening, recalling the days they chased each other as children. But this time, Dor was quiet. He carried several bowls and a jug of water. When they sat, he told Alli about Nim's visit. She began to cry.

"But where are we to go?" she said. "This is our home, our family. How will we survive?"

Dor looked down.

"Do you want me enslaved on that tower?"

"No."

"Then we have no choice."

He touched her tears and wiped them away.

"I am afraid," she whispered.

She hugged her arms around his chest and leaned her head into his shoulder. She did this every night, and like most small demonstrations of love, it had a large impact. Dor felt a surge of calm whenever she held him, like being wrapped in a blanket, and he knew no one else would ever love or understand him the way she did. He nestled his face into her long dark hair, and he breathed a way he never breathed except when he was with her.

"I will protect you," he promised.

They sat for a long while, watching the horizon.

"Look," Alli whispered. She loved the sunset colors—the oranges, the soft pinks, the cranberry reds.

Dor stood up.

"Where are you going?" Alli asked.

"I must try something."

"Stay with me."

But Dor moved to the rocks. He poured water into a small bowl, then placed a larger one beneath it. He removed a piece of clay plugged inside a hole in the upper bowl—the one Nim had mocked—and the water began to drip through, one silent splash after another.

"Dor?" Alli whispered.

He did not look up.

"Dor?"

She pulled her arms around her knees. What would become of them? she thought. Where would they go? She lowered her head and squeezed her eyes shut.

If one were recording history, one might write that at the moment man invented the world's first clock, his wife was alone, softly crying, while he was consumed by the count.

Dor and Alli stayed on the hillside that night.

She slept. But he fought his weariness to be awake when the sun rose. He watched the sky change from night black to deep purple to a melting blue. Then a burst of rays seemed to whiten everything, as the dome of the sun poked over the horizon, like the golden pupil of an opening eye.

Had he been wiser, he might have marveled at the beauty of the sunrise and given thanks for being able to witness it. But Dor was not focusing on the miracle of the day, only on measuring its length. As the sun appeared, he slid the lower bowl away from the upper bowl's dripping, took a sharp stone, and notched the waterline.

This, he concluded—this much water—was the measure between darkness and light. From now on, no one needed to pray for the sun god to return. They could use this water clock, see the level rising, and know dawn was coming. Nim was wrong. There was no divine battle between day and night. Dor had captured them both in a bowl.

He dumped the water.

God saw this, too.

Sarah is anxious.

She hurries down the steps in her still-warm black jeans. She feels a flush of panic. She remembers a night two years ago, one of the few times she's gone out with a boy. A Winter Formal dance. A kid from her math class. His hands were clammy. His breath smelled like pretzels. He left with his friends. She had to call her mother to pick her up.

This is different, she tells herself. That was a weird boy; this is a young man. He is eighteen. He is popular. Any girl at school would want him. *Look at his photo!* And he's meeting *her*!

"What time will you be back?" Lorraine asks, looking up from the couch. Her wineglass is nearly empty.

"It's Friday, Mom."

"It's just a question."

"I don't know, OK?"

Lorraine rubs her temples. "I'm not the enemy, honey."

"Didn't say you *were*."

She checks her phone. She cannot be late.

Eight-thirty! Eight-thirty!

She yanks her coat from the closet.

Victor is anxious.

He taps his fingers on the desk, waiting for Research. Grace's voice comes over the intercom.

"Honey? Are you hungry?"

"Maybe a little."

"How about some soup?"

He stares out the window. This New York penthouse is one of five homes they own. The other four are in California, Hawaii, the Hamptons, and central London. Since his cancer diagnosis, he hasn't been to any of them.

"Soup is fine."

"I'll bring it in."

"Thanks."

She has been kinder since his illness, sweeter and more patient. They have been married forty-four years. The last ten they've been more like roommates.

Victor picks up the phone to see how Research is coming. But when Grace enters with the soup, he hangs up.

Dor and Alli loaded their meager possessions on a donkey and went to live in the high plains.

Their children, it was decided, would be safer with Dor's parents. Alli was heartbroken. Twice she made Dor turn back, just so she could hug them again. When their oldest daughter asked, "Am I the mother now?" Alli collapsed, sobbing.

Their new abode was small, made of bundled reeds. It was weak against the wind and rain. Alone, without family, the couple relied solely on each other. They grew what they could, herded sheep and a single goat, and rationed water from long trips to the great river.

Dor continued his measuring, using bones, sticks, the sun, moon, and stars. It was the only thing that made him feel productive. Alli grew withdrawn. One night Dor saw her hugging their son's swaddling blanket and staring at the floor.

From time to time, Dor's father would bring them food—at his wife's insistence—and each visit, he spoke about Nim's tower, how high it had grown, how the bricks were made with fir, how the clay mortar came from the fountains of Shinar.

Already, Nim had climbed near the top, shot an arrow into the sky, and claimed it had landed with blood on its tip. The people bowed to him, believing he had wounded the gods. Soon he and his best warriors would reach the clouds, defeat whatever waited for them, and rule from above.

"He is a great and powerful king," Dor's father said.

Dor looked down. Nim was the reason they were living in exile. The reason he could not hold his children each morning. He thought about his life as a child, he and Nim and Alli running up the hills. Nim was just another man to him, really still a boy, always wanting to be the strongest.

"Thank you for the food, Father," Dor said.

"Dor. Visitors."

Alli rose to her feet. An elderly couple was approaching on foot. Many moons had now passed since Dor's banishment—on our calendar, more than three years—and Alli was grateful for any company at all. She greeted the man and woman and offered them food and water, even though there was precious little to spare.

Dor was proud of his wife's kindness. But he worried about the visitors, who did not look well. Their eyes were red and watery and their skin had dark blotches. When he was alone with Alli, he warned her, "Do not touch them. I fear they are diseased."

"They are alone and poor," she protested. "They have no one else. Show them the mercy we would want in return."

Alli served the visitors barley cakes and barley paste and the little goat's milk they had. She listened as they told their tale. They, too, had been cast out from their village, the people fearful that the dark blotches meant they had been cursed. They lived now as nomads, in a tent made of goat skins. They moved in search of sustenance and waited for the day they would die.

The old woman cried when she said this. Alli cried with her. She knew what it felt like to lose your place in the world. She held the small cup so the old woman could sip.

"Thank you," she whispered.

"Drink," Alli said.

"Your kindness . . ."

She reached out to embrace Alli, her wrinkled hands trembling.

Alli leaned in and nuzzled her cheek. She could feel the old woman's tears mixing with hers.

"Be at peace," Alli said.

As they left, Alli slipped the woman a skin filled with the last of their barley cakes. Dor checked his water clock bowl and saw a fingernail's length until the sun disappeared.

Before you measure the years, you measure the days.

And before the days, you measure the moon. Dor had done this in exile, charting its stages—full moon, half moon, quarter moon, moonless. Unlike the sun, which looked the same every day, the changing moon gave Dor something to count, and he gouged holes on clay tablets until he noticed a pattern. The pattern was what the Greeks would later call "months."

He assigned a stone to every full moon. He notched tablets for moons in between. He created the first calendar.

And now all his days were numbered.

On the fifth notch of the third stone, he heard Alli cough.

Soon her cough grew harsher, a low explosion that threw her head forward.

At first she tried to continue as usual, tending to daily tasks inside the reed house. But she grew so weak that she fell one day while preparing a meal, and Dor insisted she lie on a blanket. Perspiration beaded on her temples. Her eyes were red and teary. Dor noticed a blotch on her neck.

Inside, he was angry. He had warned her not to touch the visitors, and now they had passed on their curse. He wished they had never come.

"What should we do?" Alli asked.

Dor dabbed her forehead with the blanket. He knew they should seek out an Asu, a medicine man, who could give Alli roots or cream to make this disease go away. But the city was too far. How could he leave her? They were alone on these high plains, cut off from options.

"Sleep," Dor whispered. "You will be better soon."

Alli nodded and closed her eyes. She did not see Dor blink away his tears.

Sarah speaks to time. "Go slower," she says.

She slips out the door and heads up the street. She imagines the boy with the coffee-colored hair. She imagines him greeting her with a sudden, sweeping kiss.

She looks back and sees a light go on in her mother's bedroom. She quickens her pace. It is not beyond her mother to open the window and yell down the block. Like many teenage girls, Sarah finds her mother a huge embarrassment. She talks too much. She wears too much makeup. She is constantly correcting Sarah—*Don't slouch, Fix your hair*—when she's not complaining to friends about Sarah's father, who doesn't even live in the state anymore. *Tom did this. Tom forgot that. Tom is late on the check again.* They used to be closer, but lately mother and daughter share a mutual incomprehension; each seems baffled by the other. Sarah does not discuss boys with Lorraine; not that there has been much to discuss until now.

Eight-thirty, eight-thirty!

She hears a beep. Her cell phone.

She grabs it from her coat pocket.

Victor speaks to time. "Go faster," he says.

It has been an hour, and he is used to quick responses. It doesn't help that all around him time is literally ticking. A mantel clock sits on his desk. His computer screen clicks off the seconds. His cell phone, desk phone, printer, and DVD player all have digital time displays. On the wall is a wooden plaque with

three clocks in three time zones—New York, London, Beijing—
representing the major offices of another company he owns.

All told, there are nine different sources of time in his study.

The phone rings. Finally. He answers.

"Yes?"

"I'm faxing something over."

"Good."

He hangs up. Grace enters.

"Who was that?"

He lies. "Something for tomorrow's meetings."

"You have to go?"

"Why not?"

"I just thought—"

She stops. She nods. She takes the plates to the kitchen.

The fax machine rings, and Victor moves closer as the paper
slides through.

Dor lay on the ground beside his wife. The stars took over the sky.

It had been days since she had eaten. She was perspiring heavily, and he worried about her labored breathing.

Please do not leave me, he thought. He could not bear a world without Alli. He realized how much he relied on her from morning until night. She was his only conversation. His only smile. She prepared their meager food and always offered it to him first, even though he insisted she eat before he did. They leaned on each other at sunsets. Holding her as they slept felt like his last connection to humanity.

He had his time measures and he had her. That was his life. For as long as he could remember, it had been that way, Dor and Alli, even as children.

"I do not want to die," she whispered.

"You will not die."

"I want to be with you."

"You are."

She coughed up blood. He wiped it away.

"Dor?"

"My love?"

"Ask the gods for help."

Dor did as she asked. He stayed up all night.

He prayed in a way he had never prayed before. In the past, his faith was in measures and numbers. But now he begged the most high gods—the ones that ruled over the sun and moon—to stop everything, to keep the world dark, to let his water clock overflow. If this would happen, then Dor would have time to find the Asu who could cure his beloved.

He swayed back and forth. He repeated a whisper, "Please, please, please, please, please . . . ," squeezing his eyes shut because it somehow made the words more pure. But when he allowed his eyelids the slightest lift, he saw what he dreaded, the first change of colors on the horizon. He saw the bowl was nearly to the notch of day. He saw that his measures were accurate, and he hated that they were accurate and he cursed his knowledge and the gods who had let him down.

He knelt over his wife, her face and hair soaked with sweat, and he leaned in, put his skin on her skin, his cheek on her cheek, and his tears mixed with hers as he whispered, "I will stop your suffering. I will stop everything."

When the sun rose, he could no longer wake her.

He rubbed her shoulders. He nudged her chin.

"Alli," he whispered. "Alli . . . my wife . . . open your eyes."

She was quite still, her head limp on the blanket, her breathing feeble. Dor felt an angry surge inside him, a primal howl that began in his feet and shot up through his lungs.

"Aaaaaaaaahhhhhhhh . . ."

His cry wafted into the empty air of the high plains.

He rose, slowly, as if in a trance.

And he began to run.

He ran through the morning and he ran through the midday sun. He ran with his lungs burning, until, at last, he saw it.

Nim's tower.

It stood so tall; its peak was hidden by clouds. Dor raced toward it, obsessed with one last hope. He had watched time and charted time and measured time and analyzed time, and he was determined now to reach the only place where time could be changed.

The heavens.

He would climb the tower and do what the gods had not.

He would make time stop.

The tower was a terraced pyramid, its stairs reserved for Nim's glorious ascent.

No one dared set foot on them. Some men even lowered their eyes as they passed.

Thus, when Dor reached the base, several guards looked up, but none suspected what he would try. Before they could react, he was sprinting up the king's special steps. Slaves watched, confused. Who was this man? Did he belong? One yelled to the other. Several dropped their tools and bricks.

Quickly the slaves began ascending, too, convinced the race for the heavens had begun. The guards followed. People near the base joined in. The lust for power is a combustible thing, and soon thousands were scaling the tower's facade. You could hear a rising roar, the collective yowl of violent men, ready to take what was not theirs.

What happened next is a matter of debate.

The way history tells the story, the Tower of Babel was either destroyed or abandoned. But the man who would become Father

Time could testify to something else, because his fate was sealed on that very same day.

As the people climbed, the structure began to rumble. The brick grew molten red. A thundering sound was heard—and then the bottom of the tower melted away. The top burst into flame. The middle hung in the air, defying anything man had ever seen. Those who sought to reach the heavens were hurled off, like snow shaken from a tree branch.

Through it all, Dor climbed, until he was the only figure still clinging to the stairs. He climbed past dizziness, past pain, past his legs aching and his chest constricting. He pulled up on each step, as bodies swirled all around him. He saw glimpses of arms, elbows, feet, hair.

Thousands of men were cast from the tower that day, their tongues twisted into a multitude of languages. Nim's selfish plan was destroyed before he shot another arrow into the sky.

Only one man was allowed to ascend through the mist, one man lifted as if pulled from beneath his arms, landing on the floor of someplace deep and dark, a place no one knew existed and no one would ever find.

16

This will happen soon.

An ocean wave begins to break and a boy rises on his surf-board. He presses his toes. He steers into the curl.

The wave freezes. So does he.

This will happen soon.

A hairstylist pulls back a clump of hair and slides her scissors underneath. She squeezes. A small crunching sound.

The hair breaks free and falls towards the floor.

It stops in midair.

This will happen soon.

In a museum off the Huttenstrasse in Düsseldorf, Germany, a security guard glances at a strange-looking visitor. He is lean. His hair is long. He moves to an exhibit of antique clocks. He opens a glass case.

"No, *bi*—" the guard warns, wagging a finger, but instantly he feels relaxed, foggy, lost in thought. He thinks he sees the strange man remove all the clocks, study them, take them apart, then put them back together, an act that would take weeks.

Emerging from the thought, he finishes his word: "—*itte*."

But the man is gone.

CAVE

17

Dor awoke inside a cave.

There was no light, yet he could somehow see. There were rocky lumps beneath his feet and jagged peaks pointing down from above.

He rubbed his hands over his elbows and knees. Was he alive? How did he get here? He had been in such pain climbing the tower, but now that pain was gone. He was not breathing hard. In fact, as he touched his chest, he was barely breathing at all.

He wondered for a moment if this was a lair of the gods, and then he thought about the bodies hurled from the tower, and the bottom melting, and the promise he had made Alli—*I will stop your suffering*—and he fell to his knees. He had failed. He had not turned back the hours. Why had he left her? Why had he run?

He buried his face in his palms. He wept. The tears poured through his fingers and turned the stone floor an iridescent blue.

It is hard to say how long Dor cried.

When he finally lifted his gaze, he saw a figure sitting in front of him—the old man he had seen as a child, his chin now resting atop the staff of golden wood. He was watching Dor the way a father watches a sleeping son.

"Is it power that you seek?" the old man asked. The voice was unlike any Dor had ever heard, muted, light, as if it had never been used.

"I seek," Dor whispered, "only to stop the sun and the moon."

"Ah," the old man said. "Is that not power?"

He poked Dor's sandals and they disintegrated, leaving Dor's feet bare.

"Are you the most high god?" Dor asked.

"I am but His servant."

"Is this death?"

"You were spared from death."

"To die here instead?"

"No. In this cave, you will not age a moment."

Dor looked away, ashamed. "I deserve no such gift."

"It is not a gift," the old man said.

He rose and held his staff before him.

"You began something in your days on Earth. Something that will change all who come after you."

Dor shook his head. "You are mistaken. I am a small and shunned person."

"Man rarely knows his own power," the old man said.

He tapped the ground. Dor blinked. Before him were all his tools and instruments, his cups, his sticks, his stones and tablets.

"Did you give one of those away?"

Dor thought about the sun stick.

"One was taken," he said.

"There are many more now. Once started, this desire does not end. It will grow beyond anything you have imagined.

"Soon man will count all his days, and then smaller segments of the day, and then smaller still—until the counting consumes him, and the wonder of the world he has been given is lost."

He tapped his staff again. Dor's instruments turned to dust. The old man narrowed his gaze.

"Why did you measure the days and nights?"

Dor looked away. "To know," he answered.

"To know?"

"Yes."

"And what *do* you know . . ." the old man asked "about time?"

"Time?"

Dor shook his head. He had never heard the actual word before. What answer would suffice?

The old man held out a bony finger, then made a swirling motion. The stains from Dor's tears gathered together, forming a pool of blue on the rocky floor.

"Learn what you do not know," the old man said. "Understand the consequences of counting the moments."

"How?" Dor asked.

"By listening to the misery it creates."

He lowered his hand onto the tearstains. They liquefied and began to glow. Small wisps of smoke appeared on the surface.

Dor watched, confused and overwhelmed. He only wanted Alli, but Alli was gone. His voice choked in a whisper. "Please, let me die. I have no wish to go on."

The old man rose. "The length of your days does not belong to you. You will learn that as well."

He placed his hands together and became the size of a boy, then an infant, then he lifted like a bee taking flight.

"Wait!" Dor yelled. "How long must I be imprisoned here? When will you return?"

The old man's shrunken form reached the cave roof. It sliced a fissure in the rock. From that fissure fell a single drop of water.

"When Heaven meets Earth," he said.

And he became nothing.

18

Sarah Lemon was really good at science

and how exactly did that help her? she often wondered. What mattered in high school was popularity—based mostly on how you looked—and Sarah, who could whiz through a biology exam, disliked what she saw in the mirror as much as she figured everyone else did: the hazel eyes, too far apart, the dry, wavy hair, the gap between her teeth, the doughy flesh she had never really shed since gaining weight after her parents split up. She was big enough up top but too big on the bottom, she thought, and one of her mother's friends had said she "might grow up to be attractive" which she did not take as a compliment.

In her final year of high school, Sarah Lemon was seventeen years old and considered, by most kids, to be too smart, too weird, or both. Her classes were no challenge; she would grab desks by the windows to fight her boredom. Often she would draw in her notebook, pouty self-portraits, using her elbow to block others from seeing.

She ate lunch by herself, walked home by herself, and spent most evenings in the house with her mother, unless Lorraine had plans with the clacking women Sarah referred to as "the divorce club." Then Sarah ate alone by her computer.

Her grades ranked her third in her class, and she was waiting on an early admissions application to a nearby state university—the only school Lorraine could afford.

The application had led to The Boy.

His name was Ethan.

Tall and bony, with sleepy eyes and thick, coffee-colored hair, he was also a senior, well-liked and surrounded by male and female friends. Ethan ran on the track team. Played in a band. In the astronomy of high school life, Sarah would never have entered his orbit.

But on Saturdays, Ethan unloaded food trucks at a homeless shelter—the same homeless shelter where Sarah had been volunteering since the college application called for an essay on "an influential community experience." She'd had none up to that point, so, to fulfill the essay honestly, she offered her services and the shelter was happy to have her. True, most of the time she stayed in the kitchen, filling plastic bowls with oatmeal, because she felt self-conscious around the homeless men (a suburban girl with a down parka and an iPhone? What did she have to say to them except "I'm sorry"?).

But then Ethan arrived. She noticed him by the truck on her first day—his uncle owned a food supply company—and he noticed her, too, the only person close to his age. As he dropped a box on the kitchen counter, he said, "Hey, what's up?"

She clutched that sentence like a souvenir. *Hey, what's up?* His first words to her. Now they spoke every week. One time, she offered him a pack of peanut butter crackers from the shelf and he said, "Nah, I don't want to take food away from these people." She found that lovely, even noble.

Sarah began to view Ethan as her destiny, the way young girls often do with young boys. Far from school and its unwritten rules of who can talk to whom, she had more confidence, she stood up straighter, she left behind the social message T-shirts she sometimes wore in favor of lower-cut, more feminine tops, and she would blush when Ethan said, "Nice look today, Lemon-ade."

As the weeks passed, she grew bold enough to believe that he was feeling for her what she was feeling for him,

that this was not an accident, the two of them winding up in this unlikely place. She had read about fate in books like *Zadig* by Voltaire, or even *The Alchemist*, and she believed fate was at work here, too. Last week, she had mustered the courage to ask if Ethan wanted to hang out sometime and he'd said, "Yeah, OK, maybe Friday?"

Now it was Friday. *Eight-thirty, eight-thirty!* She tried to calm herself. She knew she shouldn't get too worked up over a boy. But Ethan was different. Ethan broke the rules of her rules.

In her raspberry T-shirt, black jeans, and heels, she'd been two blocks toward the big event when her cell phone went *Buh-duh-beep*, the sound of a text message.

Her heart jumped.

It was from him.

19

Victor Delamonte was the fourteenth-richest man in the world, according to a national business magazine.

The story ran an old photo, Victor's chin in the crook of his hand, his heavy jowls pushed up, a pensive smile on his ruddy face. It noted that "the private, bushy-browed hedge fund mogul" was an only child, born in France, who came to America and made it big, a true immigrant rags-to-riches story.

But because he refused to speak with the magazine (Victor shied from publicity) certain details of his childhood were omitted, including this: when Victor was nine, his father, a plumber, was killed in a fight in a seaside tavern. A few days later, his mother left the house wearing only a cream-colored nightgown and jumped from a bridge.

In less than a week, Victor was an orphan.

He was put on a boat to join an uncle in America. It was better, everyone thought, that the boy live in a country with fewer ghosts. Victor would later credit his financial philosophy to that ocean voyage, during which his only sack of food—three loaves of bread, four apples, and six potatoes, packed by his grandmother—was tossed into the water by some hooligan boys. He cried that night for all that he had lost, but he would say it taught him a valuable lesson: that holding on to things "will only break your heart."

So he avoided attachments, which served him well during his financial ascent. As a high schooler in Brooklyn, he purchased two pinball machines with money saved from summer jobs and he put the machines in local bars. He sold them eight months later and, with the profits, bought three candy dispensers. He sold those and bought five cigarette machines. He kept buying, selling, and re-investing until, by the time he was done with college, he owned the vending company. Soon he bought a gas station, which led him to oil, where he made numerous well-timed purchases of re-fineries that left him wealthy beyond any possible need.

He gave his first $100,000 to the American uncle who'd raised him. He reinvested everything else. He acquired car deal-erships, real estate, and eventually banks, first a small one in Wisconsin, then several more. His portfolio mushroomed, and he started a fund for people who wanted to ride his business strategy. Over the years, it became one of the highest-priced—and most sought after—funds in the world.

He met Grace in an elevator in 1965.

Victor was forty. Grace was thirty-one. A bookkeeper for his firm, she wore a modest print dress, a white sweater, and a pearl necklace, her light blond hair done up in a bouffant. Pretty, yet practical. Victor liked that. He nodded as the elevator closed and she looked down, embarrassed to be sharing such close quarters with the boss.

He asked her out through interoffice mail. They went to din-ner at a private club. They talked for hours. Victor learned that Grace had been married before, just out of high school. Her husband was killed in the Korean War. She'd buried herself in work. Victor could relate to that.

They rode a limousine to the river. They walked beneath the bridge. They shared their first kiss on a bench looking across to Brooklyn.

Ten months after their elevator encounter, they were wed in

front of four hundred guests, twenty-six from Grace's side, the
rest Victor's business associates.

At first they did so much together—played tennis, visited
museums, took trips to Palm Beach, Buenos Aires, Rome. But
as Victor's business mushroomed, their joint activities fell away.
He began to travel alone, working on the plane and even more
at his destination. They stopped playing tennis. Museum trips
grew rare. They never had children. Grace regretted that. She
told Victor so over the years. It was one of the things that led
them to talk less.

In time, the marriage felt like something spilled. Grace chafed
at Victor's impatience, his penchant for correcting people, his
reading during meals, and his willingness to interrupt any social
occasion for a business call. He disdained her minor scoldings
and how long it took her to get ready for anything, leaving him
constantly looking at his watch. They shared coffee in the mornings and the occasional restaurant at night, but as the years
passed and their wealth stacked like chips around them—multiple
homes, private jets—their life together felt more like a duty. The
wife played her role, the husband did the same. Until recently,
when, for Victor, all issues had faded behind the shadow of one.

Death.

How to avoid it.

**Four days after his eighty-sixth birthday, Victor had visited
an oncologist in a New York City hospital**

who confirmed the existence of a golfball-sized tumor near
his liver.

Victor researched every treatment option. He had always worried about bad health jeopardizing his success, and he spared no
expense in exploring a cure. He flew to specialists. He had a

team of health consultants. Despite all that, nearly a year had passed, and the results had not been good. Earlier in the day, he and Grace had seen the lead doctor. Grace tried to ask a question, but the words choked in her throat.

"What Grace wants to ask," Victor said, "is how much time do I have left?"

"Optimistically," the doctor answered, "a couple of months."

Death was coming for him.

But death would be in for a surprise.

⤞ 20 ⤝

The first voice said, "Longer."

"Who's there?" Dor screamed.

He had been trying to escape the cave since the old man left. He searched for passageways. He banged on the karst walls. He tried to lower himself into the pool of tears, but it repelled him with air, as if a million breaths were pushing up from below.

Now a voice.

"Longer," it said.

He saw only wisps of white smoke on the pool's surface, and a bright turquoise glow.

"Show yourself!"

Nothing.

"Answer me!"

Then, suddenly, there it was again. A single word. Soft, barely audible, a mumbled prayer wafting up into the cave.

"Longer."

Longer what? Dor wondered. He crouched on the floor, staring at the incandescent water, desperate, as man grows alone, for the sound of another soul.

The second voice, finally, was a woman's. It said, "More."

The third voice, a little boy's, said the same thing. The fourth—they came more quickly now—mentioned the sun. The fifth spoke of the moon. The sixth was a whisper and repeated, "more, more," while the seventh said, "another day" and the eighth begged, "go on and on."

Dor rubbed his beard, which had grown unruly, as had his hair. Despite his isolation, his body functioned normally. It was nourished without food. Replenished without sleep. Dor could walk around the cave's interior or wet his fingers with the slowly dripping water from the fissure.

But he could not escape the voices from the glowing pool—asking, always asking, for days, nights, suns, moons, and, eventually, hours, months, and years. If he put his hands over his ears, he heard them just as loudly.

And thus, unknowingly, did Dor begin to serve his sentence—

to hear every plea from every soul who desired more of the thing he had first identified, the thing that moved man further from the simple light of existence and deeper into the darkness of his own obsessions.

Time.

It seemed to be running too fast for everyone but him.

Sarah read Ethan's text on her phone.

Her heart dropped.

"Can we do this next week? Sumthin I gotta go 2 2nite. See u at shlter, OK?"

Her knees buckled, like a marionette's with the strings released. "No!" she screamed to herself. "Not next week. Now! That's what we agreed! I put on all this makeup!"

She wanted to change his mind. But a text message demanded a response, and if she took too long, he might think she was angry.

So instead of saying no, she typed: *"No problem."*

She added: *"See u at shelter."*

Then she threw in: *"Have fun."*

She pressed the send button and noted the time: 8:22.

She leaned against a traffic sign and tried to tell herself it was not her fault, he had not bailed out because she was too geeky or too fat or she talked too much or anything like that. He had something to do. It happened, right?

"Now what?" she wondered. The night was an empty crater. She could not go home. Not while her mother was still up. She had no way to explain a five-minute journey in high heels.

Instead she trudged to a nearby coffee shop and bought herself a chocolate macchiato and a cinnamon bun. She sat in the back.

"Eight twenty-two?" she said to herself. "Come on!"

But inside, she was already counting the days until next week.

❖ 22 ❖

Victor had always been able to see a problem, find its weak spot, and crack it open.

Failing companies. Deregulation. Market swings. There was invariably a hidden key; others were just missing it.

He took the same approach with death.

At first, he'd fought his cancer with conventional means—surgery, radiation, chemotherapy that left him weak and vomiting. But while these treatments had some halting effect on the tumor, his kidneys weakened, and he was forced onto dialysis three days a week, a process he tolerated only by having his chief assistant, Roger, with him the entire time, so Victor could dictate messages and be updated on business. He refused to miss a minute of the workday. He checked his watch constantly—"Let's go, let's go," he'd mumble. He hated being stuck like this. Hooked to a machine to remove waste from his blood? What kind of position was that for a man like him?

He tolerated it until he could tolerate it no more. Men like Victor looked to the bottom line, and after a year, he knew the bottom line was this:

He could not win.

Not the conventional way. Too many people had tried. It was a bad bet, hoping for a miracle.

And Victor did not make bad bets.

So he turned his attention away from the illness and focused instead on time—time running out—which was, for him, the real issue.

Like other men of enormous power, Victor could not imagine the world without him. He felt almost *obligated* to stay alive. Cancer was a stumble. But the real hurdle was human mortality.

How could he crack *that*?

He finally found his opening when a researcher from his West Coast offices, responding to his requests on "immortality," faxed a stack of material on cryonics.

Cryonics.

The preservation of humans for later reanimation.

Freezing yourself.

Victor read through the pages, then took his first satisfied breath in months.

He could not beat death.

But he might outlast it.

◆ 23 ◆

The pool of voices was formed by Dor's tears,

but he was only the first to weep. As mankind grew obsessed with its hours, the sorrow of lost time became a permanent hole in the human heart. People fretted over missed chances, over inefficient days; they worried constantly about how long they would live, because counting life's moments had led, inevitably, to counting them down.

Soon, in every nation and in every language, time became the most precious commodity. And the desire for more became an endless chorus in Dor's cave.

More time. A daughter holding her ailing mother's hand. A horseman riding to beat the sunset. A farmer fighting a late harvest. A student huddled over piles of papers.

More time. A man with a hangover smacking his alarm clock. An exhausted worker buried in reports. A mechanic under the hood with impatient customers waiting.

More time. It was the choke of Dor's existence, all he ever heard, millions of voices surrounding him like gnats. Although he'd lived when the world spoke but one language, he was granted the power to understand them all now, and he sensed by the sheer volume that Earth had become a very crowded place, and mankind did much more than hunt or build; it labored, it traveled, it made war, it despaired.

And it never had enough time. It begged Heaven to extend the hours. The appetite was endless. The requests never stopped.

Until slowly, gradually, Dor came to rue the very thing that once consumed him.

He did not understand the purpose of this slow torture, and he cursed the day he numbered his fingers, he cursed the bowls and the sun sticks, he cursed all the moments he had spent away from Alli when he could have been with her, listening to her voice, laying his head against hers.

Mostly he cursed the fact that while other men would die and meet their fate, he, apparently, was going to live forever.

THE IN-BETWEEN

✤ 24 ✤

Sarah was casual when she saw Ethan the next morning.

At least she tried to be. He was wearing a hooded sweatshirt, ripped jeans, and Nikes. He dropped boxes of pasta and apple juice on the counter.

"What's up, Lemon-ade?"

"Not much," she said, scooping oatmeal.

As he opened the boxes, she stole a few glances, hoping for clues to whatever had caused his cancellation. She wanted him to mention it—she certainly wouldn't—but he unpacked the food at his normal laconic pace and whistled a rock melody.

"That's a great song," she said.

"Yeah."

He resumed whistling.

"So what happened last night?"

Oh, God. Had she just blurted that out? *Stupid, stupid!*

"I mean, it doesn't matter," she tried to add.

"Yeah, sorry I couldn't—"

"Whatever—"

"Bad timing—"

"No, it's cool."

"Cool."

He crushed the now empty boxes and put them in the over-sized trashcans.

"You're good to go," he announced.

"Sure am."

"See you next week, Lemon-ade."

He exited the way he always did, digging his hands into his pockets and bouncing on the balls of his feet. That was it? she thought. What did he mean by *next week*? Next Friday night? Or next Saturday morning? Why didn't she ask? Why was it always up to her to ask?

A homeless man with a blue cap stepped to the window and took his oatmeal.

"Extra bananas?" he asked.

Sarah loaded his bowl—he asked the same thing every week—and he said, "Thank you," and she mumbled, "No problem," then she grabbed a paper towel and wiped around the last apple juice bottle Ethan had unpacked; the top had come loose and it had spilled all over.

25

"Inside those?" Victor asked, pointing.

"Yes," the man said. His name was Jed. He ran the cryonics facility.

Victor gazed at the huge fiberglass cylinders. They were round and fat, about twelve feet high, the color of day-old snow.

"How many people does each one hold?"

"Six."

"They're frozen in there now?"

"Yes."

"How are they . . . positioned?"

"Upside down."

"Why?"

"In case anything should happen near the top, the most important thing is to protect the head."

Victor squeezed his cane and tried to mask his reaction. As a man used to elegant lobbies and penthouse offices, he was put off by the look of this place. Located in an industrial park in a nondescript New York suburb, it was a single-level brick building with a loading dock on the side.

Inside was equally unimpressive. A small set of rooms in the front. A lab where the bodies began the freezing process. A big open warehouse where the cylinders stood side by side, six people per unit, like an indoor cemetery with linoleum floors.

Victor had insisted on visiting the day after he received the reports. He had stayed up all night, skipping his sleeping pills, ignoring the pain in his stomach and back. He'd read everything twice. Although it was a relatively new science (the first person cryogenically frozen was in 1972), the thinking behind cryonics was not illogical. Freeze the dead body. Wait for science to advance. Unfreeze the body. Bring it back to life and cure it.

The last part, of course, would be the trickiest. But look at how mankind had advanced during *his* lifetime, Victor figured. Two of his childhood cousins had died of typhoid and whooping cough. Today, they'd have lived. Things changed. "Don't get too attached to anything," he reminded himself, including accepted knowledge.

"What's that?" he asked. Near the cylinders, a white wooden box, partitioned by numbers, held several bouquets of flowers.

"For when family members come to visit," Jed explained. "Each number corresponds to a person in a cylinder. The visitors sit over there."

He pointed to a mustard-colored couch, pushed against the wall. Victor tried to picture Grace sitting in such a ratty thing. It made him realize he could never tell her about this idea.

She wouldn't accept it. Not a chance. Grace was a steadfast churchgoer. She did not believe in meddling with fate. And he was not about to argue with her.

No. This final plan would be up to him. We are, as we die, who we most were in life, and since he was nine years old, Victor had been accustomed to doing for himself.

He made a mental note: No visitors. No flowers. And pay whatever it took to get his own cylinder.

If he were going to wait centuries to be reborn, he would do it alone.

26

All caves begin with rain.

The rain mixes with gas. The new acidic water eats through rocks, and tiny fractures grow into passageways. Eventually— after many thousands of years—these passageways might create an opening large enough for a man.

So Dor's cave was already a product of time. But inside, a new clock was ticking. From the ceiling, where the old man had cut a fissure, the dripping water gradually formed a stalactite.

And as that stalactite dripped onto the cave floor, a stalagmite began to rise.

Over the centuries, the two points grew toward each other, as if drawn by magnets, but so slowly that Dor never took notice.

Once, he had prided himself on keeping time with water. But man invents nothing God did not create first.

Dor was living in the biggest water clock of all.

He never thought about this. Instead, he stopped thinking altogether.

He stopped moving. He no longer stood up. He put his chin in his hands and held still amid the deafening voices.

Unlike any man before him, Dor was being allowed to exist without getting older, to not use a single breath of the numbered breaths of his life. But inside, Dor was broken. Not aging is not the same as living, and without human contact, his soul dried up.

As the voices from Earth increased exponentially, Dor heard them without distinction, the way one hears falling raindrops.

His mind dulled from inactivity. His hair and beard grew comically long, as did the nails of his fingers and toes. He lost any concept of his own appearance. He had not seen his image since he and Alli went to the great river and smiled at their reflection in the water.

He wanted desperately to hold on to every memory like that. He squeezed his eyes shut to recall every detail. Until finally, at some unmarked point in his purgatory, Dor shook the lethargy of his darkness, sharpened the edge of a small rock, and began to carve on the walls.

He had carved on Earth

but always as a form of timekeeping, counting, notching moons and suns, the earliest math in the world.

What Dor carved now was different. First he made three circles to remember his children. He gave each of them a name. Then he carved a quarter moon to remind him of the night he told Alli, "She is my wife." He carved a box shape to remind him of their first home together—his father's mud-brick house—and a smaller box to symbolize the reed hut they shared.

He drew an eye shape to remind him of Alli's lifted gaze, the look that made him feel tipped over. He drew wavy lines to suggest her long dark hair and the serenity he felt when he buried his face inside it.

With each new carving, he spoke out loud.

He was doing what man does when left with nothing.

He was telling himself his own life story.

27

Lorraine knew there was a boy involved.

Why else would her daughter have worn heels last night? She only hoped Sarah hadn't picked a jerk like her father.

Grace knew Victor was frustrated.

He hated to lose. And it saddened her that this last fight, against a terminal illness, was destined to be a defeat.

Lorraine heard the front door open, and Sarah, without a word, whisked upstairs to her room.

It was how life worked between them now. They lived together but apart.

Things were different even a few years ago. When Sarah was in eighth grade, a girl in gym class stuffed a volleyball under her shirt and, unaware Sarah was within earshot, cooed to a group of boys, "Hey, guys, I'm Sarah Lemon, can I have your French fries?" Sarah raced home crying and buried herself in her mother's lap. Lorraine stroked her hair and said, "They should all be expelled, every one of them."

She missed being of comfort like that. She missed the way they once leaned on each other. She heard Sarah moving about upstairs and wanted to speak with her. But the door was always closed.

Grace heard Victor return from his outing.

"Ruth, he's home," she said into the phone, "let me call you back."

She came to the door and took his coat.

"Where were you?"

"The office."

"You had to go on Saturday?"

"Yes."

He hobbled down the hallway, still using his cane. She didn't ask about the manila folder under his arm. Instead she said, "Do you want some tea?"

"I'm all right."

"Something to eat?"

"No."

She remembered a time when he'd kiss her at the door, lift her a few inches off the ground and spoil her with questions like "Where do you want to go this weekend? London? Paris?" Once, on the balcony of a seaside villa, she said she wished she'd met him earlier in life, and he said, "We're gonna make up for that. We're gonna live a long time together."

She reminded herself there were moments like that once, and that she had to be patient now, more compassionate; she could not know what he was feeling inside—the dwindling days, the impending death. However cranky or distant he got, she was determined to make the little time they had left more like the start of their life together, and less like the vast, joyless middle.

She did not know, as Victor disappeared into his study, that he was thinking about another life altogether.

28

Mankind is connected in ways it does not understand—even in dreams.

Just as Dor could hear voices from souls he could not see, so, too, on occasion, could a sleeping man or woman see his image from beyond.

In the seventeenth century, a portrait of Queen Elizabeth featured a skeleton looking over one shoulder, and an old, bearded man looking over the other. The skeleton was meant to represent death, but the mysterious bearded figure was, the artist claimed, a symbol of time that had come to him in a dream.

A nineteenth-century etching depicted another bearded man, this one holding an infant, symbolizing the New Year. No one knows why the artist chose this image. He also told colleagues he had seen it in a dream.

In 1898, a bronze sculpture showed a more robust man, still bearded but bare-skinned and fit, holding a scythe and an hourglass and positioned over a giant clock in a rotunda. The model for this bearded man remains a mystery.

But he was referred to as "Father Time."

And Father Time sits alone in a cave.

He holds his chin in his hands.

This is where our story began. From three children running up a hillside to this lonely space, a bearded man, a pool of voices, the stalactite now within a millimeter of the stalagmite.

Sarah is in her room. Victor is in his study.
It is this time. Right now.
Our time on Earth.
And Dor's time to be free.

FALLING

29

"What do you know about time?"

Dor looked up.

The old man had returned.

On our calendar, it had been six thousand years. Dor gaped in disbelief. When he tried to speak, no sound came forth; his mind had forgotten the pathway to his voice.

The old man stepped quietly about the cave, examining the walls with great interest. On them he saw every symbol imaginable—circle, square, oval, box, line, cloud, eye, lips— emblems for each moment Dor recalled from his life. *This is when Alli threw the stone . . . This is when we walked to the great river . . . This is the birth of our son . . .*

The final symbol, in the bottom corner, was the shape of a teardrop, to forever remind Dor of the moment Alli lay dying on the blanket.

The end of his story.

At least to him.

The old man bent down and stretched out his hand.

He touched that carved teardrop, and it became an actual drop of water on his finger.

He moved to where the stalactite and stalagmite had grown to within a razor's edge of each other. He placed the teardrop between them and watched it turn to stone, connecting the two formations. They were one column now.

Heaven meets Earth.

Just as he had promised.

Instantly, Dor felt himself rise from the floor, as if being pulled by strings.

All his carved symbols lifted off the wall, moving across the cave like migrating birds, then shrinking into a tiny ring around the narrow throat that joined the rocky shapes together.

With that, the stalactite and stalagmite crystallized into smooth, transparent surfaces—forming an upper bulb and a lower bulb— the shape of a giant hourglass.

Inside was the whitest sand Dor had ever seen, extremely fine, almost liquid-like. It spilled through from top to bottom, yet the sand in each bulb neither grew nor diminished.

"Herein lies every moment of the universe," the old man said. "You sought to control time. For your penance, the wish is granted."

He tapped his staff on the hourglass and it formed a golden top and bottom with two braided posts. Then it shrank into the crook of Dor's arm.

He was holding time in his hands.

"Go now," the old man said. "Return to the world. Your journey is not yet complete."

Dor stared blankly.

His shoulders slumped. Once, the very suggestion would have sent him running. But his heart was hollow. He wanted none of this anymore. Alli was gone, she would always be gone, a teardrop on a cave wall. What purpose could life—or an hourglass— serve him now?

He brought a sound up from his chest and, in a faint whisper, finally spoke.

"It is too late."

The old man shook his head. "It is never too late or too soon. It is when it is supposed to be."

He smiled. "There is a plan, Dor."

Dor blinked. The old man had never used his name before.

"Return to the world. Witness how man counts his moments."

"Why?"

"Because you began it. You are the father of earthly time. But there is still something you do not understand."

Dor touched his beard, which reached his waist. Surely he had survived longer than any man. Why was life not finished with him yet?

"You marked the minutes," the old man said. "But did you use them wisely? To be still? To cherish? To be grateful? To lift and be lifted?"

Dor looked down. He knew the answer was no.

"What must I do?" he asked.

"Find two souls on earth, one who wants too much time and one who wants too little. Teach them what you have learned."

"How will I find them?"

The old man pointed toward the pool of voices. "Listen for their misery."

Dor looked at the water. He thought about the billions of voices that had wafted up through it.

"What difference could two people make?"

"You were one person," the old man said. "And you changed the world."

He picked up the stone that Dor had used for his carvings. He crushed it into dust.

"Only God can write the end of your story."

"God has left me alone," Dor said.

The old man shook his head. "You were never alone."

He touched Dor's face and Dor felt new spirit filling his body, like water being poured into a cup. The old man began to fade away.

"Remember this always: There is a reason God limits man's days."

"What is the reason?"

"Finish your journey and you will know."

30

After Ethan's cancellation, Sarah might have thought twice about another date.

But a desperate heart will seduce the mind. And so, two weeks after the disappointment of the black-jeans-and-raspberry-T-shirt night, two weeks' worth of boring science classes and nights eating dinner in front of the computer, Sarah tried again. She got up extra early on a shelter Saturday, 6:32 A.M., and dressed as if she were going to a party. She wore a low-cut blouse and a skirt that was just tight enough. She spent extra time on her face, even checking a few websites that gave tips on blush and eye shadow. She felt awkward, considering all the times she'd criticized her mother's heavy makeup ("It's like you're screaming for attention," Sarah would complain), but she justified her efforts because a boy like Ethan could have beautiful girls anytime, girls with even more makeup and even lower-cut blouses. If she wanted him, she had to change some habits.

Anyhow, Lorraine was still sleeping.

So Sarah slipped out, took her mother's car, and drove to the shelter, feeling OK with her decision, until a few of the homeless men saw her, whistled, and said, "You look *fine*, young miss," and she blushed and made up a story about an event she was going to later, and suddenly she felt ridiculous. What was she thinking? She was not the kind of girl who could pull this off. Luckily, she'd brought a sweater. She yanked it on.

And then Ethan entered, a box under each arm. Caught off-guard, Sarah straightened up and ran a hand through her hair.

"Lemon-*ade*," he said, nodding.

Did he like this look?

"Hi, Ethan," she said, trying to be casual, but feeling a rush all over again.

31

Victor sat at his desk, looking through the manila folder. He remembered what Jed, the cryonics man, had said two weeks ago.

"Think of the freezing as a lifeboat to the future—when medicine is so advanced, curing your disease will be as simple as making an appointment.

"All you have to do is get in the lifeboat, go to sleep, and wait for the rescue."

Victor rubbed his abdomen. To be rid of this cancer. To be free of dialysis. To live all over. *As simple as making an appointment.*

He reviewed the process as Jed had explained it. The moment Victor was declared dead, his body would be covered in ice. A pump would keep his blood moving so it wouldn't clot. Next, his bodily fluids would be replaced with cryoprotectant—a biological antifreeze—so that no ice could form inside his veins, a process called "vitrification." As its temperature was continually lowered, his body would be placed inside a sleeping bag, then a computer-controlled cooling box, then a container where liquid nitrogen was gradually introduced.

After five days, he would be moved to his final resting place, a giant fiberglass tank called a "cryostat"—also filled with liquid nitrogen—and lowered in headfirst, where he would remain suspended for, well, who knew?

Until his lifeboat found the future.

"So my corpse stays here?" Victor had asked Jed.

"We don't use the word 'corpse.'"

"What word do you use?"

"'Patient.'"

Patient.

It was easier when Victor thought of it that way. He was already a patient. This was just a different kind. A patient being patient. Like waiting on a long-range stock fund or enduring a negotiation with the Chinese, who always insisted on endless levels of paperwork. Patient. Although Grace might disagree, Victor could be patient when he had to be.

And being frozen for decades, maybe centuries, in exchange for coming out the other side, ready to resume his life—well, that didn't seem a bad trade.

His time on Earth was almost up.

But he could grab new time.

He dialed a number on his phone.

"Yeah, Jed, this is Victor Delamonte," he said. "When can you come by my office?"

32

In the immeasurable centuries he spent inside the cave, Dor had tried every form of escape.

Now he stood, the hourglass in his arms, and waited by the edge of the pool. He somehow knew this was his only way back.

Could this really be over? he thought. This endless purgatory? What kind of world awaited him now? The Father of Time had no idea how long he'd been away.

He thought about what the old man had said. *Listen for their misery.* He looked down at the glowing surface, shut his eyes, and heard two voices rise above the din, an older man and a younger woman:

"Another lifetime."

"Make it stop."

Suddenly, a wind roared through the cave, and the walls lit as if splashed by a midday sun. Dor clasped the hourglass to his chest, stepped back, and leapt into the air above the pool, whispering the only word that ever truly gave him comfort.

"Alli."

He fell right through.

Dor descended in open air.

His legs flipped over his head, then his head back over his legs, and he dropped quickly into a gleaming mist filled with light and colors. He saw fleeting views of bodies and faces, the men being shaken off of Nim's tower; only they were going up and he was going down. He tightened his grip on the hourglass and sped into brighter light and deeper colors, the wind piercing his flesh like the blades of a rake, until he was sure he was being torn apart by the sheer velocity. He fell through bracing cold and searing heat, through blowing rain and swirling snow and then sand, sand, pelting sand, whipping sand, spinning him and cushioning him and finally dropping him the way sand dropped through his hourglass, a straight line until he came to a stop.

The sand blew away.

He felt himself hanging from something.

He heard distant music and laughter.

He was back on Earth.

EARTH

33

Lorraine needed cigarettes.

She pulled into a strip mall and passed a nail salon. She remembered taking Sarah here once, when she was eleven.

"Can I have ruby-red polish?" Sarah asked.

"Sure," Lorraine said. "How about your toes?"

"I can do them, too?"

"Why not?"

Lorraine watched Sarah's amazed expression as a woman placed her feet in a small tub of water. She realized how little anyone doted on her daughter, what with Lorraine working and Tom always getting home late. When Sarah turned to her, beaming, and said, "I want whatever color toes you're getting, Mom," Lorraine vowed that they would do this more often.

They never did. The divorce changed everything. Lorraine walked past the salon window and saw many empty chairs, but she knew Sarah would rather be arrested these days than sit next to her mother for a manicure.

Grace needed groceries.

She could have written a list, sent someone from the staff. "You don't need to do chores," Victor always told her. But over time, she realized the tasks that swallowed many people's days only left a hole in hers. Gradually, she took them back.

She moved her cart up the supermarket aisles now, taking celery, tomatoes, and cucumbers from the produce department. In the last few months she had resumed cooking to prepare healthy

meals for Victor—nothing processed, everything organic—
hoping to buy him more time through a better diet. It was a
small gesture, she knew, a stick against the wind. But all she had
to cling to was hope.

A healthy salad tonight, she told herself. But as she passed the
ice cream freezer, she grabbed a pint of mint chocolate chip, Victor's favorite. If he wanted a moment's indulgence, she would
have that ready, too.

⊰ 34 ⊱

It was a December festival in a small Spanish town.

Street musicians gathered in the plaza, amid tables loaded with *tapas* of shrimp, anchovies, potatoes. A fountain in the plaza's center contained coins thrown by hopeful lovers. Visitors sat on the edge and dangled their feet in the water.

Hanging near that fountain, from a plywood base, was a life-sized papier-mâché mannequin of a bearded man holding an hourglass. EL TIEMPO, the sign read. FATHER TIME. Beneath it was a plastic yellow bat.

Every few minutes, someone walked by and swatted the mannequin with that bat. It was tradition. Whack out the old year, welcome in the new. Onlookers yelled, "Ooyay! Ooyay!" and laughed and toasted.

A little boy broke free of his mother's grip and ran to the mannequin. He lifted the bat and looked for approval.

"OK . . . OK . . . ," his mother yelled, waving.

Just then, the sun emerged from behind a cloud, and a strange light cloaked the village. A sudden wind blew sand across the plaza. The boy paid it no mind. He brought the bat around full force on the papier-mâché figure.

Whack!

Its eyes opened.

The boy screamed.

Dor, hanging from a plywood wall, felt a twinge in his side.

His eyes opened.

A little boy screamed.

The scream so jolted Dor that he jerked backward and his robe ripped off two nails from which it hung. He fell to the ground, dropping the hourglass.

The boy's scream suddenly stopped. Actually it held and faded, like a long trumpet note. Dor scrambled to his feet. The world around him had just slowed to a dreamlike state. The boy's face was locked in mid-scream. His yellow bat hung in the air. People at a fountain were pointing but not moving.

Dor picked up the hourglass.

And he ran.

At first, he ran as fast as he could,

keeping his head down, hoping no one would notice him. But he was the only thing moving. The whole world had been paused. No wind blew. No tree branches swayed. People Dor saw appeared nearly frozen—a man walking a dog, a group of friends holding drinks outside a bar.

Dor slowed. He looked around. By our standards, he was on the rural outskirts of a small Spanish village, but to him, there were more people and structures than he had seen in his lifetime.

Herein lies every moment of the universe, the old man had said. Dor observed the sand in the hourglass. It, too, had slowed to a near stop, only a few grains dripping through, as if someone had choked the flow.

Dor walked for miles, holding that hourglass. The sun barely moved in the sky.

His shadow followed behind him, although all other shadows seemed to be painted on the ground. When he reached a more deserted area, he climbed a hillside and sat. Climbing made him think of Alli, and he longed for that old world—the empty plains, the mud-brick homes, even the quiet. In this world he heard a constant hum, as if a hundred sounds were being mashed into one note. He didn't yet know this was the sound of a single slowed moment.

Down below Dor saw a stretch of road, straight and charcoal-colored with a white stripe down its center. He wondered how many slaves were needed to build such a smooth surface.

You sought to control time, the old man had said. *For your penance, the wish is granted.*

Dor thought about his arrival on Earth, how he had fallen and dropped the hourglass. That was when everything changed.

Perhaps . . .

He turned the hourglass sharply to the side, then back again.

The sand began to flow freely. The humming stopped. He heard a *whoosh*. Then another. He looked down and saw cars speeding along the road—only he had no concept of cars, so he could only imagine they were beasts of some unimaginable speed. He quickly snapped the hourglass back.

The cars stopped in place.

The hum returned.

Dor's eyes widened. Had he just done that? Brought the world to a near standstill? He felt a surge of power so great, it made him shiver.

The night started awkwardly, but the alcohol changed that.

Ethan brought a bottle of vodka. Sarah acted nonchalant. Although she was in no way a drinker, she quickly took a sip. Even a girl ranked third in her class academically knows enough to pretend she's had vodka before.

They sat in his uncle's warehouse—Ethan's idea, since he didn't really commit to the evening until 8:14 P.M., by texting, "*Over at my uncle's if u want 2 come*"—and they drank from paper cups and mixed in orange juice that Ethan grabbed off the shelf. Sitting on the floor, they laughed about a dumb TV show they both confessed to watching. Ethan also liked action movies, especially the *Men in Black* series, where the actors wore suits and ties and sunglasses, and Sarah said she liked those movies, too, although truthfully she hadn't seen them.

She wore the same low-cut blouse she had worn the morning at the shelter, figuring he must have liked it, and he did seem attentive. At one point her phone rang (her mother, *God!*) and when she made a face, Ethan said, "Lemme see." He took her phone and programmed a special ring tone, a shrill, heavy-metal music lick, that would signal whenever her mom was calling.

"You hear her, you ignore her," he said.

Sarah laughed. "Oh, that is *so* great."

After that, things got blurry. He offered to rub her back and Sarah gladly accepted; his hands on her shoulders made her shiver then melt. She tried talking, nervously, about how she didn't really have friends at school because they all seemed so immature, and he said yeah, a lot of those kids were losers, and she said she was stressed over getting into college, and he rubbed her shoulders deeper and said she was smart enough to get in anywhere, which made her feel good.

And then the kiss. She would never forget that. She felt his breath on the nape of her neck and she turned to the left, but he edged onto her right, so she turned back that way and their faces nearly bumped—and it happened. It just happened. She closed her eyes and honestly, she almost fainted (her mother used to say the word "swoon," and Sarah had a vague idea this was that), and he kissed her again, harder, and turned her toward him and grabbed her closer, and she remembered thinking *Me, he's kissing me, he wants me!* But what started softly got a little rough, his hands moved quickly all over her, until she nervously pulled away and then, embarrassed, tried to laugh it off.

He filled her cup with more vodka and orange juice, and she gulped it faster than she should have. The rest of the night she remembered laughing and pushing Ethan and him pulling and them kissing again, and Ethan getting more aggressive and her pulling away and drinking and repeating the pattern.

"Come on," he said.

"I know," she murmured. "I want to, but . . ."

Ultimately, he backed away and drank more vodka, until he almost fell asleep against the wall. Not long after that, they each went home.

But now she wondered,

chewing the crust of her whole wheat toast on a Monday morning—7:23 A.M.—if she had done the right thing, the wrong thing, or the wrong thing by doing the right thing. She realized Ethan was a better-looking boy than she was a girl, and she pondered how much "gratitude" she was supposed to show him for that. They'd kissed—a lot—and he'd wanted her. *Somebody wanted her.* That was what mattered. She kept seeing his face. She pictured the next time they'd be together. Finally, something to look forward to in her drab and ordinary existence.

She put her plate in the sink and flipped open her laptop. She was going to be late for school—Sarah was never late for school—but Christmas was coming and she had a sudden urge to buy Ethan a present. He'd said the actors in *Men in Black* wore these special, cool-shaped watches. Maybe she could buy him one. He would like that, wouldn't he? Something only she would think of?

She told herself she was just being thoughtful. Christmas was Christmas. But deep in her heart, the equation was simple.

She would buy a present for the boy she loved.

And he would love her back.

36

Can you imagine having endless time to learn?

If you could freeze a moving car and study it for hours? Wander through a museum touching every artifact, the security guards never knowing you were there?

That is how Dor explored our world. Using the power of the hourglass, he slowed time to suit his needs. Although he could never stop it completely—a train might move an inch in the hours he spent investigating it—he could easily hold people in place while he circulated through them, touching their coats or their shoes, trying on their eyeglasses, rubbing the clean-shaven faces of men, so different from his time, when long beards were common. These people would remember nothing of his presence, only the quickest flicker across their field of vision.

Dor wandered the Spanish countryside this way, living days inside a moment, exploring neighborhoods, cafes, stores. He found clothes that fit his frame (he preferred the type you pulled on, as buttons and zippers perplexed him), and at one point he wandered into a low-level brick building marked PELUQUERÍA, a hair salon. He looked into a long mirror and yelled out loud.

Only then did he realize he was seeing his reflection.

Dor had not seen himself in six thousand years.

He moved closer to the mirror, alongside a businessman in a high, spinning chair and a female stylist with her hands in a drawer. Dor observed the man's reflection—blue suit, maroon tie, hair short, dark, and wet—and then he looked at his own unruly image. Despite his massive beard and flowing hair, he appeared to be younger than the businessman next to him.

In this cave, you will not age a moment.

I deserve no such gift.

It is not a gift.

He stepped back, crouched behind a counter, and tilted the hourglass.

Life resumed. The stylist removed scissors from the drawer and said something that made the businessman laugh. She lifted his hair and began to cut.

Dor peeked over the counter, fascinated. She moved so adeptly, the scissors snipping, the locks of hair falling. Suddenly, someone turned on a stereo and music blasted, a thumping beat. Dor clamped his hands over his ears. He had never heard anything so loud.

He looked up to see a fat, middle-aged woman, with her hair in plastic curlers, standing over him, staring.

"*¿Qué quiere?*" she yelled.

Dor grabbed his hourglass and she—and everyone else—slowed to a near-freeze.

He rose, walked around the woman (her mouth still open), and went to the stylist. He took the scissors from her hand, put the blades near the bottom of his beard, and began to cut away six thousand years of hair.

37

"I asked you here because I want to change the rules."

Victor poured Jed a glass of ice water. They sat across a long table. Victor was reluctantly using the wheelchair now (his walking had grown too unsteady), and the office furniture had been rearranged for clear maneuvering.

"Under the law, I must be legally dead before the freezing process can begin, correct?"

"That's right," Jed answered.

"But you agree—science agrees—that if the freezing could start before the heart and brain gave out, the chances of preservation would be that much better."

"In theory . . . yes." Jed palmed the glass. He seemed leery.

"I want to test that theory," Victor said.

"Mr. Delamonte—"

"Hear me out."

Victor explained his plan. Dialysis was the only thing keeping him alive. The big machine that washed his blood and removed the toxins. If he stopped treatment, he would die in a short time. Days, perhaps. A week or two at most.

"The moment I died, a doctor would confirm system failure, a coroner would confirm death, and the freezing would begin, right?"

"Yes," Jed said, "but—"

"I know. We would all have to be at your site when it happened."

"Right."

"Or *before* it happened."

"I don't follow."

"*Before* it happened . . ." He let the words sink in. "To say it already *had* happened."

"But to do that, they would have to . . ."

Jed stopped. Victor jiggled his jaw. He believed the man was beginning to understand.

"When you have a lot of money," Victor said, "you can get people to do things." He crossed his hands. "Nobody has to know."

Jed stayed quiet.

"I've seen your facility. It's pretty—don't take this the wrong way—bare bones?"

Jed shrugged.

"You could use a few million dollars, no? A bequeathal from a satisfied customer?"

Jed swallowed.

"Look," Victor said, lowering his voice to a friendlier tone. "I'll already be near death. What difference could a few hours make?

"And let's be honest." He leaned in. "Wouldn't you like to see your chances of success improve?"

Jed nodded.

"So would I."

Victor steered his wheelchair over to his desk. He opened a drawer.

"I've had my legal guys draw something up," he said, lifting an envelope. "I'm hoping this helps you make up your mind."

38

With his trimmed hair and modern clothes, Dor looked more like he belonged in this century,

and as he studied the world, he manipulated the hourglass to allow short bursts of real-time interaction. He used these mostly for essential stepping stones—like learning the alphabet, which he accomplished in the back of an adult education language class. The alphabet led to spelling, the spelling to words, and since Father Time could already understand any tongue on Earth, his mind did the rest.

Once he could read, all knowledge was within reach.

He immersed himself in a library in Madrid, reading more than a third of the volumes. He read history and literature, studied maps and oversized photo books. With the hourglass turned, this took mere minutes, although in real time, decades would have passed.

When he emerged from the library, Dor turned the hourglass again to see the night fall. He watched in awe at how electricity— which he had read about—elongated man's waking hours. Dor had only known lighting from oil lamps or fire. Now streetlights kept towns awash in illumination, and Dor walked beneath them in their pools of yellowish-white. He stayed up all night, staring at the bulbs in utter fascination.

In the morning, he paused the sun once again

and wandered across the Spanish plains, along the largest river in France, and through the forests of Belgium and Germany. He saw ancient ruins and modern stadiums, explored skyscrapers, churches, shopping centers.

Wherever he went, Dor sought out timepieces. The old man had been right. Dor may have been the world's first time keeper, but humanity had taken his simple stick and bowl concepts and developed them into an endless array of devices.

Dor familiarized himself with all of them. In a Düsseldorf museum on the Hutterstrasse, he took apart every antique clock in the exhibit, studying the springs and coils while the frozen security guard stood a few feet away. In a Frankfurt flea market, he found a clock radio that, when you held down buttons, allowed time to flip forward or back. Dor pressed the backward button, watching time diminish, Wednesday, Tuesday, Monday, thinking how nice it would be if he could just hold it down until he landed back home.

You are the father of earthly time.

Could he really be responsible for all this? Dor thought about the centuries he had been made to suffer in the cave. He wondered if every clock watcher pays some kind of price.

Finally, Dor reached the coast.

He came upon a lighthouse in Westerhever, Germany. He had read about lighthouses and the great North Sea. He turned his hourglass to watch the waves break. Then he turned it back.

His education concerning the modern world was complete. Dor had spent one hundred years observing a single day.

He listened to the wind. He heard what he needed to hear.

"Another lifetime."

"Make it stop."

He waded into the still water.

And began to swim.

39

Dor swam the Atlantic Ocean. He did it in a minute.

When he left Germany, it was 7:02 P.M. When he reached Manhattan, it was 1:03 P.M. He had technically, on our clocks, swum back in time.

As he churned through the water—unaffected by cold or fatigue—he let his mind wander through all he had seen and the people from his life to whom he had never said good-bye, people now gone for thousands of years. His father. His mother. His children. His beloved wife.

Finish your journey and you will know.

He wondered when that would be. He wondered what he had to learn. Mostly he wondered, as he crossed the ocean one stroke at a time, when he would get to die like everyone else.

Upon reaching land, Dor pulled himself up the side of a shipping dock.

A dockworker with a cap and thick stubble spotted him. "Hey, pal, what the hell—"

He got no further.

Dor turned the hourglass. He gazed up at a massive skyline and realized he was in the strangest place yet.

New York City loomed as an unimaginable metropolis,

even after all Dor had seen in his one hundred years of study in Europe. The buildings were taller, with barely a breathing space between them. And the people. The sheer *number* of them!

Bunched at street corners. Spilling out of storefronts. Even with the entire city slowed by his power, Dor had trouble weaving through the bodies.

He needed clothes, so he took pants and a black turtleneck from a shop named Bravo! He found a coat that suited him on a hanger in a Japanese restaurant.

As he walked between the massive skyscrapers, he was reminded of Nim's tower. He wondered if there were no end to man's ambitions.

CITY

40

The hands of a clock will find their way home.

This was true the moment Dor marked his first sun shadow.

As a child sitting in the sand, he had predicted that tomorrow would contain a moment like today, and the next day a moment like tomorrow. Every generation after Dor was determined to sharpen his concept, counting ever more precisely the measure of their lives.

Sundials were placed in doorways. Giant water clocks were constructed in city squares. The move to mechanical designs—weight-driven, verge and foliot models—led to tower clocks and grandfather clocks and eventually clocks that fit on a shelf.

Then a French mathematician tied a string to a timepiece, put it around his wrist, and man began to wear time on his body.

Accuracy improved at a startling rate. Although it took until the sixteenth century for the minute hand to be invented, by the seventeenth century, the pendulum clock was accurate to within a minute a day. Less than one hundred years later, it was within a second.

Time became an industry. Man divided the world into zones so that transportation could be accurately scheduled. Trains pulled away at precise moments; ships pushed their engines to ensure on-time arrivals.

People awoke to clanging alarms. Businesses adhered to "hours of operation." Every factory had a whistle. Every class-room had a clock.

"What time is it?" became one of the world's most common

questions, found on page one of every foreign-language instruction book. *What time is it? ¿Qué hora es? Skol'ko syejchas vryemyeni?*

No surprise then that when Dor, the first man to truly ask that question, reached the city of his destiny—where the voices behind *"Another lifetime"* and *"Make it stop"* wafted in the wind—he used his knowledge to secure work in the one place time would always be around him.

A clock shop.

And he waited for two hands to come home.

41

Victor's limo eased through lower Manhattan.

It turned down a cobblestone street, where, tucked into a curve, was a narrow storefront. A strawberry-colored awning carried the street address, but there was no name on the place, only a sun and a moon carved into the front door.

"One Forty-Three Orchard," the driver announced.

Two of his workers exited first and lifted Victor into his wheelchair. One held the door open as the other pushed him through. He heard the hinges creak.

Inside the air felt stale and preserved, as if from another era. Behind the counter stood a pale, elderly, white-haired man with a plaid vest and blue shirt, a pair of wire-rim glasses halfway down his nose. Victor figured him for German. He had a good eye for nationalities, with all the traveling he had done.

"*Guten tag*," Victor offered.

The man smiled. "You are from Germany?"

"No, just guessed that you were."

"Ah." He lifted his eyebrows. "What can we find for you?"

Victor rolled closer, observing the inventory. He saw every kind of clock—grandfather clocks, mantel clocks, kitchen clocks with swinging glass doors, lamp clocks, school clocks, clocks with chimes and alarms, clocks in the shape of baseballs and guitars, even a cat clock with a pendulum tail. And the pendulums! On the wall, on the ceiling, behind glass, swaying back and forth, tick tock, tick tock, as if every second of the place moved to the left or the right. A cuckoo bird emerged, whirring levers announcing its arrival, followed by eleven cuckoos over eleven bells. Victor watched the bird slide back behind its door.

"I want the oldest pocket watch you have," he said.

The proprietor smacked his upper lip.

"Cost?"

"Doesn't matter."

"All right . . . One moment."

He moved to the back and mumbled something to someone.

Victor waited. It was December, a few weeks before his final Christmas, and he'd decided to buy himself a timepiece. He would have the cryonics people stop it the moment he was frozen; when he reached the new world, he would start it up again. He liked symbolic gestures like that. Anyhow, it was a good investment. An antique today would be worth much more centuries from now.

"My apprentice can help you," the proprietor said.

From the back stepped a man whom Victor guessed to be in his mid-thirties, leanly muscled, his dark hair mussed and uneven. He wore a black turtleneck. Victor tried to guess his nationality. Strong cheekbones. Somewhat flattened nose. Middle Eastern? Maybe Greek?

"I'm looking for the oldest pocket watch you have."

The man closed his eyes. He appeared to be thinking. Victor, never a patient man, glanced at the owner, who shrugged.

"He is very knowledgeable," the proprietor whispered.

"Well, let's not take a lifetime," Victor said. He chuckled to himself. "Or another lifetime."

Another lifetime.

The man's eyes popped open.

42

Ethan hadn't seemed as attentive the next week at the shelter.

Sarah told herself it could be anything. Maybe he was tired. As a gag, she wrapped a pack of peanut butter crackers with a little red bow. Privately, she was hoping for a kiss. But when Ethan saw it, he smirked and said, "All right, thanks."

She hadn't mentioned their night together, because she didn't know what to say. She was embarrassed to admit that, thanks to the alcohol, she didn't remember every detail (she, Sarah Lemon, who once memorized entire verses of *The Canterbury Tales* for English class), and besides, she thought less was more when it came to talking about that night.

Instead she tried to make more topical conversation, about all the things she felt they had in common, as they had done before things got physical. But something was off. Whatever subject she raised, Ethan ended with a clipped response.

"What's wrong?" she finally asked.

"Nothing."

"You sure?"

"I'm just beat."

They fell into silence and unpacked the boxes. Eventually, Sarah blurted out, "That vodka was good," but it sounded as phony as it felt. Ethan grinned and said, "Can't lose with booze," and Sarah laughed, but too loudly.

As he left, Ethan lifted a hand and said, "See you next week." She was hoping he would add "Lemon-ade"; she just wanted to hear him say it, but when he didn't, she heard herself say,

"Lemon-ade" and then she wondered, *Oh, God*—had that been out loud?

"Yeah. Lemon-ade," Ethan said. He walked out the door.

That afternoon, without a word to her mother, Sarah withdrew money from her bank account and took an hour-long train into New York City to buy his special watch.

Sometimes, when you are not getting the love you want, giving makes you think you will.

43

Victor had to admit, that apprentice knew what he was doing.

He'd located a timepiece made in 1784, a pocket watch trimmed in eighteen-karat gold, with a painted shell depicting three people under the stars—a father, mother, and child. The dial was white enamel and had lifted Roman numerals. The hands were silver. The mechanics were the old-fashioned verge fusee system. It even made small chiming sounds on the hour. Given its age, the watch was in excellent condition.

Coincidentally, it had been made in France.

"I was born there," Victor said.

"I know," the apprentice said.

"How would you know?"

The apprentice shrugged. "Your voice."

His voice? Victor didn't have an accent. He thought about it, then let it go. He was more interested in the timepiece, which fit perfectly in his palm.

"Can I take it with me?"

The apprentice looked to the proprietor, who shook his head. "We'll need a few days to ensure its operation. Remember, this is a very old piece."

Sitting now in the back of the limo, Victor realized they had never told him what the watch cost.

Not that it mattered. He hadn't asked the price of anything in a long time.

He swallowed several pills and drank the rest of a ginger ale.

The pain around his stomach and kidneys was throbbing, as it had been for months. But the dread he felt in his time running out was being addressed the way he always addressed things: with methodical action.

He checked his watch. This afternoon, he would consult with his legal team. Then he'd review the cryonics documents. Finally, he'd go home to Grace, who would be waiting with another of her "healthy" meals—bland and tasteless vegetables, no doubt. It was typical of the gap between them, he thought. Here she was trying to stretch his meager days, while he was planning for another century.

He thought again about the pocket watch, how perfectly it had fit in his palm. He was surprised at how energized he was from the purchase, even though it was another thing he couldn't tell Grace about.

44

The newscaster was talking about the end of the world.

Sarah stepped closer to the TV in the train station. The man was discussing how, according to Mayan calendars, the world was scheduled to end next week. Some predicted a spiritual awakening. Others saw Earth's collision with a black hole. In various corners of the world, people were gathering in churches, squares, fields, near the ocean, awaiting the end of existence.

She thought of telling this to Ethan. She thought of telling everything to Ethan. She pulled out her phone and texted him.

"Did u hear Tuesday is end of the world?"

She pressed send and waited. No reply. Probably had his phone off. Or in his pocket.

The train came and she boarded. She had most of her savings account in her purse—seven hundred and fifty-five dollars—and she wondered how much a movie watch would cost.

◈ 45 ◈

Although it was the weekend, Victor's office was brimming with activity.

An expression at his firm went: "If you don't come in on Saturday, don't bother coming in on Sunday."

Victor nodded to various employees as Roger wheeled him down the halls. Roger, tall and pale, with cheeks that sagged like a hound dog's, was almost always by Victor's side. He was unfailingly loyal, never questioning an instruction, and Victor rewarded him handsomely.

"Afternoon," Victor mumbled as Roger pushed him into the conference room, where five lawyers gathered around a long rectangular table. The winter sun sliced through the window shades.

"So. Where are we?"

One lawyer leaned forward, pushing a pile of papers.

"It's incredibly complicated, Victor," he said. "We can only set up documents based on current law."

"Future rulings could render them obsolete," added another.

"Can't protect against everything," said a third.

"Depends on how long we're talking," said the first.

"Normally, your estate would pass to Grace," the fourth lawyer said.

Victor thought of her again, how she knew nothing of this plan. He felt a pang of guilt.

"Go on," he said.

"But if we do that, she controls everything. And when she

goes, to return it to you, well, the law is fuzzy on leaving an estate back to someone who is already, technically . . ."

Everyone looked around.

"Dead?" Victor said.

The lawyer shrugged. "It's better to set up certain funds right now, insurances, a special trust—"

"—a dynasty trust," the first lawyer interjected.

"Right. Like the kind you use for a great-grandchild's education. This way the money can revert to you when you are . . . what's the right word?"

"Revived?"

"Yes, revived."

Victor nodded. He was still thinking about Grace, how much he would set aside to take care of her. She always said she didn't marry him for his money. Still, how would it look if he didn't leave more than enough for her every need?

"Mr. Delamonte," the third lawyer asked, "when are you planning the . . . uh . . ."

Victor snorted a breath. Everyone had such a hard time with the word.

"I should be gone by the end of the year," he said. "Isn't that to our benefit?"

The lawyers looked at one another.

"It would make the paperwork easier," one said.

"By New Year's Eve, then," Victor announced.

"That's not much time," one lawyer protested.

Victor wheeled to the window and looked out over the rooftops.

"That's right," he said. "I don't have much time—"

He leaned forward and stared in disbelief. There, on a skyscraper just across the street, was a man, sitting on the ledge, his feet dangling. He was cradling something in his arms.

"What is it?" one of the lawyers asked.

"Some lunatic with a death wish," Victor said.

Still, he couldn't turn away. It wasn't concern over the man falling. It was the fact that he seemed to be looking straight into Victor's window.

"So. Should we start with the commodities portfolio?" one lawyer said.

"Huh? . . . Oh. Yes."

Victor lowered the shade and returned to the business of how much he could take with him when he died.

46

Sarah stood outside the clock shop, looking at the sun and moon that were carved into the door.

She figured this must be the place, even though there was no name on the front.

She stepped inside and felt as if she'd entered a museum. *Oh, God, they won't have it*, she told herself. *Look at this old stuff.*

"Can I help you?"

The proprietor reminded her of a chemistry teacher she'd had sophomore year, with white hair and narrow glasses. He'd worn vests, too.

"Do you carry—you probably don't—but there's this watch, I think. I don't even know if they make it, but . . ."

The old man held up a palm.

"Let me get someone who will know," he said.

He returned from the back with a serious-looking guy, mussed brown hair, a black turtleneck. Kind of handsome, Sarah thought.

"Hi," Sarah said.

He nodded, wordlessly.

"It's a watch from a movie. You probably don't have it . . ."

Ten minutes later, she was still explaining.

Not so much about the watch, but about Ethan and why she thought this would make a good gift. The guy behind the counter was easy to talk to; he listened with a patience that made it seem as if he had forever (his boss must be pretty lenient, she thought), and since she didn't talk to her mother about Ethan, and she couldn't confide in anyone at school (Ethan hadn't told anyone, so she followed his lead), it was a relief, almost fun, to let someone in on the relationship.

"He's kind of quiet sometimes," she said, "and he doesn't always text back."

The man nodded.

"But I know he likes this movie. And the watch was like, a triangle, I think? I want to surprise him."

The man nodded again. A cuckoo clock sounded. Because it was five o'clock, it went on for five chimes.

"Ooohh, enough," Sarah said, putting her hands to her ears. "Make it stop."

The man flashed a look as if she were in danger.

"What?" Sarah said.

The cuckoo finished.

Make it stop.

There was an awkward silence.

"Um . . . ," Sarah offered, "if you show me some watches, maybe I can tell you if it's the right one?"

"Good idea," the proprietor interjected.

The man went to the back. Sarah drummed her fingers on the counter. She saw an open jeweled case near the cash register, with an old pocket watch inside, painted on the exterior. It looked expensive.

The man reemerged, holding a box. On the cover was a photo from the *Men in Black* movie.

"Ohmigod, you have it?" Sarah said excitedly.

He handed her the box and she opened it. Inside was a sleek black watch in the shape of a triangle.

"Yes! I am so happy."

The man tilted his head. "Then why are you so sad?"

"Huh?" Sarah squinted. "What do you mean?"

She looked to the proprietor, who seemed embarrassed.

"He's very good at what he does," he whispered, apologetically.

Sarah tried to shake off the question. Who said she was sad? It was none of his business how she felt.

She looked down and saw a price on the box. Two hundred and forty-nine dollars. She felt suddenly uncomfortable and wanted to get out of there.

"All right, I'll buy it," she said.

The man looked at her sympathetically.

"Ethan," he said.

"What about him?"

"Is he your husband?"

"*What?*" she squealed. She found herself smiling. "No! God. I'm a senior in *high school*."

She brushed back her hair. Her mood suddenly lightened. "I mean, we might get married one day, I guess. But now he's just . . . my boyfriend."

She had never used that word before, and she felt a bit self-conscious, as if walking out of a fitting room in a short skirt. But the man smiled, too, and she forgave him that weird comment about her being sad, because it fit beautifully, that word, "boyfriend," and she wanted to say it again.

47

Every evening, when the sun set in New York City, Dor ascended to the top of skyscrapers and sat on their ledges.

He would turn the hourglass and hold the metropolis in a creeping moment, silencing the traffic noise into a single blaring hum. With the darkening sky behind the countless tall buildings, he'd imagine Alli at his side, the way they used to sit watching the day come to a close. Dor had no need for sleep or food. He seemed to be living on a different time grid altogether. But his thoughts were as they always had been, and when he finally let the darkness fall, he pictured Alli again, wearing her veil, and the quarter moon of the night they wed.

She is my wife.

He missed her terribly, even after all this time, and he wished he could talk to her about this mysterious journey, ask her what fate awaited him at the end. He had found the two people he was sent to Earth to find—or they had found him—but he still did not understand why a man in a wheelchair and a lovestruck girl should be singled out from the masses.

He held the hourglass close to his face to see the symbols he had carved during his purgatory,

the symbols which had lifted from the walls and engraved the ring between the upper and lower bulbs. With his power over time, Dor could have taken anything he desired from this new world. But a man who can take anything will find most things unsatisfying. And a man without memories is just a shell.

And so, there, alone, high above the city, Father Time held the only possession he cared about, the hourglass with his story. And, once again, out loud, he recited his life:

"This is when we ran up the hillside . . . This is the stone Alli threw . . . This is the day we were wed . . ."

48

Victor looked at the two needles. He exhaled.

He had been doing dialysis for nearly a year. He hated it more each time he went. From the day a graft was placed under his skin, and a half-inch tube protruded from his arm, he'd felt imprisoned, an animal in a net. Three visits a week. Four hours per visit. The same dull routine. Watch the blood exit and return.

He had fought them on the idea, fought them on the graft, and refused to be with other patients during his treatments, even though Grace agreed with the doctor who said, "It helps to talk with people facing the same challenge." To Victor, they were not facing the same challenge: They were staying alive for another month or year; he was plotting an entirely new life.

He paid for a private suite—equipped with computers and an entertainment center—and he paid for private nurses. With Roger only a few feet away, Victor used the four hours to work, keeping a remote keyboard propped above the blanket, his BlackBerry on the table, and his cell phone connected via a device on his ear.

A nurse entered now with her clipboard.

"How we doing today?" she asked Victor. She was red-haired and overweight and her outfit tugged in from the bust and waist.

"Just peachy," he mumbled.

"That's good," she said.

He looked past her, tired, and drifted into a dreamy state. Another week of this, he thought. After that, he would disengage and be on that boat to the new world by New Year's Eve.

He blinked at a shadow in the corner, the size of a man, but when he blinked again, it was gone.

The shadow was Dor.

He'd been exploring the building in his undetected way—wandering among the machines and the staff, trying to comprehend the process that, despite his prolonged observation, still mystified him. Somehow, this place healed the sick. That he understood. And he felt a familiar twinge of sadness he experienced whenever he witnessed modern medicine: Alli had died alone, on a blanket in the high plains. Had she been of this generation, might she not have lived a long life?

He wondered how it was fair that your dying should depend so much on when you were born.

Dor studied the large machine in the private suite, saw how blood made its way in and out of the body. He approached Victor, sitting in the large chair with a device in his ear—Victor, whose fate Dor would have to address to reach his own destiny.

How old was this Victor, who, like Nim, seemed to be treated better than other people? Based on the wrinkled flesh, thinned hair, and age spots on his arms, he seemed to have already been blessed with long years. Yet Dor noticed Victor's expression—his eyebrows furrowed, his lips pulled down at the sides.

Although a diseased man might be frightened—or even grateful—this one seemed . . . *angry*.

Or a better word.

Impatient.

49

Now that Sarah had Ethan's gift, she needed only a time and place to give it to him.

She kept texting him, but he didn't respond. Maybe his phone was broken. But how else to reach him? There were only a few school days before the Christmas break. Finding him in the crowded hallways was chancy. Besides, she followed his lead at school and never spoke to him. The relationship was their little secret.

She knew that after classes he had indoor track practice. So she decided to wait outside the gym and "accidentally" bump into him. Standing in the hallway, holding the wrapped present, she looked away as the other kids passed—the "hot" girls in their designer clothes; the thick, sculpted jocks; the hipsters in black-framed glasses and funky hats; the sour-faced, deeply emotional types in ragged black T-shirts and studded earrings. Some of them she had seen for four years without exchanging a word. But that was how high school worked; it issued a verdict and you behaved accordingly. The verdict on Sarah Lemon was too smart, too fat, too weird—so few kids bothered to talk to her. She had been counting down the months to graduation until Ethan came along. Ethan, amazing Ethan, who dared to defy her verdict. He wanted her. *Someone wanted her.* She felt so grown-up now, having him as a boyfriend. She wanted to brag.

She spotted two girls she had known since the third grade—Eva and Ashley—walking toward her in clingy striped tops and the kind of tight jeans Sarah could never squeeze into. They glanced her way and she reflexively looked at her feet. Inside she was yelling, *Guess who I'm waiting for?* But then her phone rang—the harsh, heavy-metal guitar riff, the ring tone signaling her mother—and as Sarah quickly flicked it silent, she heard Eva and Ashley laughing.

She suddenly felt self-conscious being there, and she put Ethan's gift inside her coat pocket and left. He'd never believe it was an accident anyhow, and she'd have no explanation besides the truth: that she was now, literally, chasing after him.

When she got outside, she texted him again.

50

Victor wheeled into his private office and pushed the door shut behind him. Only then did he see the apprentice from the clock shop, standing against the wall.

"How did you get in here?" Victor asked.

"Your timepiece is ready."

"Did my secretary let you in?"

"I wanted to bring it to you."

Victor paused. He scratched his head. "Let me see."

The apprentice reached into his bag. Such an odd guy, Victor thought. If he worked for me, he'd be in the lab, one of those shy, nerdy technicians who one day invents a product that turns the company into a gold mine.

"Where did you learn so much about timepieces?" Victor asked.

"It was once an interest of mine."

"Not anymore?"

"No."

He opened a box and handed over the pocket watch, its jeweled case polished to a shine.

Victor smiled. "You really buffed this up."

"Why do you want such a device?"

"Why?" Victor exhaled. "Well. I have a journey coming up, and I'd like to have a sturdy timepiece with me."

"Where are you going?"

"Just some R and R."

The man looked lost.

"Rest and relaxation? You do come out of that back room once in a while, don't you?"

"I have been other places, if that is what you mean."

"Yes," Victor answered. "That's what I mean."

Victor examined his visitor. Something was off about him. Not his clothes so much. But his language. He got the words right, but they didn't fit naturally, as if he were borrowing them from a book.

"The other day, in the shop, how did you know I was from France?"

The man shrugged.

"You read it somewhere?"

He shook his head.

"The Internet?"

No response.

"I'm serious. Tell me. How did you know I was from France?"

The man looked down for several seconds. Then he flashed his eyes straight at Victor.

"I heard you ask for something when you were a child. Then, as now, you wanted time."

51

Sarah got the idea from, of all people, her mother.

Lorraine, over a dinner of chicken pot pies, was talking about a bracelet she and her friends were buying for a woman who was turning fifty. They were having it engraved with a message.

As soon as Lorraine said that, Sarah thought of Ethan. A message on the back of his watch? Why hadn't she thought of that?

"Sarah? Are you listening?"

"What? Yeah."

The next day, Sarah cut her last two classes (again, uncharacteristic for her, but she had Ethan now, and he required time, too) and took the train back to the city. When she entered the clock shop, it was late afternoon, and she was once again the only customer. She felt sorry for this place, because if it wasn't busy at Christmas, when would it be?

"Ah," the old proprietor said, recognizing her. "Hello again."

"You know the watch I got here?" Sarah said. "Can you engrave it? Do you do that?"

The proprietor nodded.

"Great."

She took the box from her bag and put it on the counter. She looked through the door that led to the back room.

"Is the other man here?"

The proprietor smiled.

"You want him to do it?"

Sarah flushed. "Oh, no. I mean, I didn't know if he did it or not. Whoever. I mean. Yeah. If he does it. Sure. But anybody can."

Privately, she was hoping the man *was* there. He was, after all, the only person she'd told about Ethan.

"I'll get him," the proprietor said.

A moment later, Dor emerged from the back, wearing the familiar black turtleneck, his hair still mussed.

"Hey," Sarah said.

He looked at her with his head tilted slightly. He had the gentlest expression, Sarah thought.

He picked up the watch.

"What do you want it to say?" he asked.

She had chosen a simple message.

She cleared her throat.

"Can you put . . ." She lowered her voice to a near-whisper, even though no one else was in the shop. " 'Time flies with you'?"

Dor looked at her, puzzled.

"What does it mean?"

Sarah raised her eyebrows. "Is it too serious? Honestly, I think—this sounds stupid, right?—I think he's like, the one for me. But I don't want to overdo it."

Dor shook his head. "The phrase. What does it mean?"

Sarah wondered if he was kidding. "Time flies? You know, like, time goes really fast and suddenly you're saying good-bye and it's like no time passed at all?"

His eyes drifted. He liked it. "Time flies."

"With you," she added.

52

Even after the funeral, young Victor wondered if his father might return one day, magically,

as if all this—the priest, the weeping family, the wooden casket—was just some phase you went through when adults had accidents.

He asked his mother. She said they should pray. Perhaps God knew a way they could all be together. They knelt by a small fireplace, and she pulled a shawl over their shoulders. She closed her eyes and mumbled something, so Victor did the same. What he said was, "Please make it yesterday, when Papa came home."

In a cave, far away, the boy's words wafted up through a glowing pool. There were millions of other voices, but the pleas of a child find our ears differently, and Dor was moved by the simple request. Children so rarely ask to reverse time. Mostly they are in a hurry. They want a school bell to ring. A birthday to arrive.

"Please make it yesterday."

Dor remembered Victor's voice. And while they deepen with age, voices are, to one destined to listen for eternity, as distinct as a fingerprint. Dor knew it was him the moment Victor spoke in the shop.

He did not know that the child who had asked for yesterday was now seeking to own tomorrow.

Victor never prayed again.

Once his mother leapt from that bridge, he gave up on prayer, he gave up on yesterdays. He came to America and learned that those who made the most of their time prospered. So he worked. He sped up his life. He trained himself not to think about his younger days.

Now, in his top-floor office, he was being reminded of them by a virtual stranger.

"I heard you ask for something when you were a child," the apprentice said. "Then, as now, you wanted time."

"What are you talking about?"

The apprentice pointed to the pocket watch.

"We all yearn for what we have lost. But sometimes, we forget what we have."

Victor looked at the timepiece, the painting of the family.

When he looked up, the man had vanished.

Victor yelled, "Hey!" assuming it was some trick. "Hey! Get back here!"

He rolled his wheelchair to the door. Roger was already headed his way, as was Charlene, his executive assistant.

"Is everything OK, Mr. D?" Charlene said.

"Did you see a guy just run out of here?"

"A guy?"

He noticed the concerned look on her face.

"Forget it," he said, embarrassed. "My mistake."

He shut the door. His heart was racing. Was his mind going now? He felt uncharacteristically out of control.

The phone rang, jolting him. His private line. It was Grace, asking when he was coming home. She was cooking.

He exhaled.

"I don't know if I can eat that stuff, Grace."

"Just come home and we'll see."

"All right."

"Is something wrong?"

Victor looked at the pocket watch. He found himself thinking about his parents, seeing their faces, something he had not done in years. It made him angry. He needed to get back on track.

"I'm stopping the dialysis, Grace."

"What?"

"It's pointless."

"You can't."

There was a long pause.

"If you do that . . ."

"I know."

"Why?" her voice was shaky. He could tell she was crying.

"It's no way to live. I'm on a damn machine. You heard what the doctors said."

She was breathing hard.

"Grace?"

"Just come home and we can talk about it, OK?"

"My mind is made up."

"We can talk about it."

"OK, but don't fight me on this." He would have preferred to use this sentence regarding his real plan—to freeze his way into another life. But he already knew she'd have no part of that. So he said it now, a true sentence for a false reason.

"I don't want to fight," she whispered. "Just come home."

53

It was set. Ethan would meet her Christmas night

at Dunkin' Donuts, because she knew it would be open. The plan had come together by accident—although Sarah chose to view it as fate.

She'd had no luck reaching him via text. But upon leaving the clock shop, she had walked past another "End of the World" gathering, and as any idea sparked the adjacent idea of calling Ethan, she dialed his number impulsively, even though he almost never answered his phone.

When she heard him say hello, her heart caught in her throat. She quickly blurted out, "You'll never guess what I'm looking at."

"Who's this?"

"Sarah."

Pause. "Hey, Sarah. I thought I dialed . . . this phone is screwed up."

"Guess where I'm calling from?"

"I don't know."

"The 'End of the World' table in Washington Square Park."

"That's crazy."

"I know, right? Anyhow, they say the world is going to end next week, and I have something I want to give you, so I better do it fast."

"Wait. What's the end-of-the-world part?"

"I don't know, it's Indian or religious or whatever. One of those freakoid things."

She had read more but didn't want to sound too smart. When had being smart ever gotten her anywhere with boys?

"So when can we get together? I want to give you this thing."

"You don't need to give me anything, Sarah."

"It's no big deal. Christmas, right?"

"Yeah. I don't know . . ."

There was an awkward pause, and Sarah felt her stomach tighten.

"It won't take long."

"All right," he said.

"Can't take long if the world is gonna end, right?"

"I hear ya." It didn't sound as if he heard her at all.

They settled on Christmas night at the Dunkin' Donuts—he had a party to go to near there anyhow—and she hung up and was glad to have something on the schedule. She tried to ignore his distracted tone, figuring phones were never a good barometer of anything. Besides, once he saw the watch, he'd be happy. No one else would be giving him a gift that special.

She thought back to him kissing her. He wanted her. *Someone wanted her.* This time around, she told herself, she would be more relaxed about the whole physical thing. She'd let him do more. He'd be happy about that, too. It was fun thinking about making him happy.

She glanced at the crowd of doomsday gatherers, some with signs, some dressed in religious clothing. On one table, a set of small speakers was playing a song that caught Sarah's ear.

Why does the sun go on shining?
Why does the sea rush to shore?
Don't they know—it's the end of the world
'Cause you don't love me anymore?

Depressing, she thought. And kind of cynical for this event. Still, the female singer's voice was so sad and melancholy that she found herself listening longer.

Why do the birds go on singing?
Why do the stars glow above?
Don't they know—it's the end of the world? . . .

She picked up a pamphlet from the table. On the front it read, "The End is coming. What will you do with the time you have left?"

Well, it was only Wednesday. She was going to lose a pound or two.

54

Grace waited for Victor to come home.

She wiped her eyes. She cut the vegetables.

Lorraine waited for Sarah to come home.

She vacuumed. She smoked a cigarette.

This will happen soon.

Every person on the planet—including Grace, Lorraine, Victor, and Sarah—will instantly stop aging.

And one person will start.

LETTING GO

Victor had done his homework. He knew what dying would entail.

Once he stopped dialysis, his blood pressure zoomed, he grew puffy, his back hurt, and his appetite disappeared. He'd anticipated these symptoms, and he forced himself to ingest bread, soup, and supplements, because he didn't want to weaken too soon.

On Christmas, he was moved from the wheelchair to a bed in the living room. Grace stayed with him all night, sleeping in a chaise. She had accepted his untrue plan for the very reasons he knew she would not accept his true one—letting go was natural, embracing God's will. If he was at peace with stopping the dialysis, then she could be, too.

Still, she hid a tear the next morning when Victor asked Roger to bring over a set of files. *Don't be mad*, she told herself now, as she bent a straw for him into a glass of water, *this is how he holds on to his life, his papers, his business, it is who he is.* She didn't know that Roger was bringing documents to protect Victor's future empire.

She offered him the glass, which Victor took himself, rather than let her hold it for him. He sipped the water then put the glass down. He saw the concern on her face.

"It's OK, Grace. It's the way it's supposed to be."

It was not, in the world's design, the way it's supposed to be.

Not this. Not freezing yourself for a second go-round. But Victor was determined to control his dying the way he'd controlled his living. The numbness coming in his feet and hands? His skin turning a sickly gray? Both would be identified as end-stage signs of renal failure. Death would be expected. No one would suspect an alternative plan—Victor being frozen *before* he died. When that happened, only Roger, Jed, and a carefully chosen doctor and coroner would be present, and all would be well paid for their silence.

Death, on paper, would come when they wrote it came.

But death would never touch Victor.

He would duck it. And jump a boat to the future.

"Listen, Grace," he said, his voice scratchy. "I know how hard this has been. But once I'm gone, everything is taken care of. All the paperwork, I mean. Roger can go over everything with you. What's important is . . ."

He thought about what to say next. He wanted it to be true.

"What's important is, you'll never have to worry."

Her eyes watered.

"I was never worried," she said.

She took his hand. She stroked his fingers.

"I'm going to miss you, you know."

He nodded.

"Terribly," she added.

Each of them squeezed their lips tightly and Victor swallowed hard. He almost told her everything right then, that very moment. But you grab a moment, or you let it pass.

He let it pass.

"Me, too," he said.

56

Ethan was, in her mind, the only boy she would ever love. But he did not love her back.

That became clear on Christmas night in the parking lot of Dunkin' Donuts when, at 9:16 P.M., offering a brightly wrapped box containing an engraved watch from his favorite movie, Sarah finally blurted out how she felt about him, something she had been holding inside like an exploding star, something she had only told the man in the clock shop and the mirror in her bedroom. But before she finished, before she said the last words of "I just really—I know it's crazy—I just *love* you, you know?" he began rolling his eyes as if he were looking for some friend to say, "Can you believe this?"

She wanted to melt into the ground at that moment, just hot wax into a puddle and disappear through a sewer grate. His eyes. That look. No interest. Total humiliation. The minutes of awkward talk from then until he said, "Look, Sarah, I gotta go" felt like years. She wanted to explain it better, erase the words. She could wait, she could wait forever. *Just don't ruin it, don't end it!* But when he gave her back the present, still wrapped, and he walked away and dug his hands into his pockets and then half a block down he took out his phone to call—who? Some other girl? Some friend to share a private laugh about this idiot who just told him he was (did she really say this?) her "ideal"? *God, Sarah, what is wrong with you?* After that, she turned to a new companion in the parking lot, invisible to all but her, a devil, a misery beast, who put his bony claw around her and said, "You live with me now."

Sarah Lemon was only seventeen, but at that moment, she began to disengage from life. She felt alone, abandoned. And it was all her fault. How could she have blown something that rare, a boy like Ethan who had never looked at her before and would never look at her again? They had kissed and he had wanted her, but she had pushed him off and he'd obviously decided she wasn't worth the bother—which she'd known all along she wasn't—and why hadn't she just shut up and done whatever he desired, who was she saving herself for, honestly, like someone better was going to come along?

Dizzy, her stomach tight, she slipped the gift back into her coat pocket. She wanted desperately to call him, but it suddenly hit her—she couldn't call him, she couldn't see him; it was over, totally over, and she fell to the ground like a dropped sack of rice. She cried on her knees until her chest hurt from heaving. She felt gravel in her palms from pressing on the asphalt. She remained on all fours until a man from the Dunkin' Donuts pushed the door open and yelled, "Hey, what you doing out here? Go someplace else!" She wobbled to her feet. She staggered forward. A heart weighs more when it splits in two; it crashes in the chest like a broken plane. Sarah dragged her wreckage back to the house, up to her bedroom, and down into a deep dark hole.

Dor sat on a skyscraper, his feet dangling. The city below was a massive array of rooftops, spires, and window lights.

He held the hourglass. He did not turn it. He let time pass at its normal pace, thinking about what the old man had instructed.

He had found the two people. He had followed them in recent days. He had paused the world around Sarah and Victor many times, trying to understand their lives. He gathered that Victor, for all his wealth, could do little to stop his illness. And by the way Sarah collapsed in the parking lot, she cared for the tall boy more than he cared for her.

But the complexity of their worlds was baffling. Dor came from a time before the written word, a time when if you wished to speak with someone, you walked to see them. This time was different. The tools of this era—phones, computers—enabled people to move at a blurring pace. Yet despite all they accomplished, they were never at peace. They constantly checked their devices to see what time it was—the very thing Dor had tried to determine once with a stick, a stone, and a shadow.

Why did you measure the days and nights?
To know.

Sitting high above the city, Father Time realized that knowing something and understanding it were not the same thing.

No morphine. Not yet. Victor needed to keep control.

His breathing had accelerated, as his body tried to exhale carbon monoxide fast enough to battle its growing acidity.

It would not be long now.

A small number of visitors—mostly business associates—came to pay final respects. Others wanted to, but Victor told Grace he wasn't up to their good-byes; that was true, but mostly because he didn't feel like he was going anywhere. Other people's dying weeks are filled with fear or farewells; Victor's had been consumed with planning. He had his exit strategy. And it now included this detail:

Each year, on New Year's Eve, Victor and Grace traditionally attended a gala in which they presented a large donation to their charitable foundation. The amount reflected the success of Victor's fund that year.

"Grace, you should go," he'd said yesterday.

"No."

"You need to present the check."

"I won't leave you."

"It will mean a lot to everybody."

"Someone else can do it."

He lied one more time.

"It would mean a lot to me."

She was surprised. "Why?"

"Because I want the tradition to go on. I want you to do it this year, next year, hopefully many more."

Grace hesitated. The gala had been her idea. Victor had never been crazy about it—he'd even fought her about going in years past. She wondered if, in some way, this was her husband saying "I'm sorry."

"All right," she said. "I'll go."

He nodded as if relieved. "It'll be good for everybody."

59

Sarah awoke at two in the afternoon, with Lorraine banging on the door.

"Sarah!"

". . . What? . . ."

"Sarah!"

"I'm up!"

"I've been banging for five minutes!"

"I had headphones on!"

"What's going on?"

"Nothing!"

"Sarah!"

"Leave me alone!"

She heard her mother walk away, then fell back into the pillow and groaned. Her head hurt. Her mouth felt like cotton. Lorraine had thankfully been out when she'd returned home last night, and Sarah had snuck two of her sleeping pills before locking the bedroom door. Now, with her head pounding, she flopped over and relived everything in her mind—what she said last night, what Ethan said. She began to cry when she saw his wrapped package sitting on her chair. She reached for it, threw it against the wall, and cried even harder.

She thought about him walking away. She felt so helpless. That couldn't be the end. That couldn't be their last time together. There had to be something she could do . . .

Wait. Maybe she could write him. Take everything back.

Make an excuse. The gift was a gag. She'd been drunk. Problems at home. Whatever. She could control things better in writing, couldn't she? Not make the same mistakes, not blurt out all those words that scared him?

She wiped her eyes.

She sat down at her desk.

Common sense would have told Sarah to steer clear of Ethan's waters. But common sense has no place in first love and never has.

She would not send a text.

She didn't want this popping up on his cell phone. But she could send a private Facebook message. She gripped the edge of her desk, thinking of what to say.

She would start with, "Listen, I'm sorry . . ." and then she'd go into how she understood why he was put off, how she sometimes got way too deep about things, and how, well, whatever she would say—as long as she didn't take herself too seriously, maybe he wouldn't, either.

She turned on her computer.

The screen lit up.

Once, lovers on faraway shores sat by candlelight and dipped ink to parchment, writing words that could not be erased.

They took an evening to compose their thoughts, maybe the next evening as well. When they mailed the letter, they wrote a name, a street, a city, and a country and they melted wax and sealed the envelope with a signet ring.

Sarah had never known a world like that. Speed now trumped the quality of words. A fast send was most important. Had she lived in an older, slower world, what happened next would not have happened. But she lived in this world.

And it did.

She went to his Facebook page.

Up came his picture, all that coffee-colored hair, the sleepy eyes, the grin that said "mildly amused." But before she could click to send him a message, her eyes found his latest post. They blinked. They welled with tears. A sick feeling began to spread inside her. She read it twice. Three times. Four times.

"Sarah Lemon made play 4 me. Whoa. Ain't happening. That's what u get 4 being nice."

Suddenly, she couldn't swallow. She couldn't breathe. If the room had caught fire, she'd have burned to a crisp, because she could not lift her body from the chair. Her stomach felt as if it were tying itself around a pole and pulling from both ends.

"Sarah Lemon made play 4 me."

Her name was on his page.

"Whoa. Ain't happening."

An unwelcome cat, trying to crawl into his lap.

"That's what u get 4 being nice."

That was it? He was being *nice*?

She shivered. She hyperventilated. Beneath his post was a long row of faces, people commenting—dozens of them.

"Seriously?" one read.

"U + Sarah = gross."

"C movie: he's just not into u."

"That butt's too big, bro."

"Knew she was a skank."

"Run, dude!"

It was like one of those dreams where you are naked on a stage and everyone is pointing. Ethan had told the world, the world sympathized, and Sarah Lemon was now and forever (because wasn't cyberspace instantly forever?) someone you had to be *nice* to, a pathetic girl who just didn't get it, the scourge of her generation, the lowest rung on the ladder, a loser.

"Sarah Lemon made play 4 me."

For him? But hadn't he been kissing her?

"Whoa. Ain't happening."

Was she that disgusting?

"That's what u get 4 being nice."

Was it charity? The beautiful taking pity on the ugly?

"Isn't she the science geek?"

"Never be nice to psychos."

"She's delusional."

"2 bad, Ethan."

Sarah slammed the computer shut. She heard the expulsion of her breath—exhale, exhale, exhale. Then she raced downstairs and burst out the front door, the thumbnail faces in an orbit around her brain, laughing at her misery, flipping open previous rejections like the worn pages of a familiar book. She was fatty Sarah again, running home from school after a girl made fun of her. She was unlovable Sarah again, whose father didn't want her after the divorce. She was geeky Sarah again, in the corner of the lunchroom with a science book. Now she was delusional Sarah, crazy stalker Sarah, a post on Ethan's Facebook page, a joke being slapped from computer to computer like one of those beachballs at a concert that never touches the ground.

She ran, shivering, in lightly falling snow, tears streaming down her face and hardening in the cold. There was no one to talk to. No one to comfort her. There was blackness and solitude and she was never, ever going back to that school again. *What should she do? What should she do?*

She thought for the first time about killing herself, the when and the how.

She already had the why.

NEW YEAR'S EVE

⋦ 60 ⋟

It was 8 P.M. Grace dressed before the mirror.

She didn't want to go. She would say her hellos, present the check, and return quickly. Her makeup was done. Her hair was set. Her dress needed to be zipped, something Victor had always done for her. She reached around awkwardly, fumbling several times. But on the third try, her fingers found the zipper, and she pulled it up successfully. Then she burst into tears.

She went to the kitchen, poured some cold ginger tea, wiped her eyes, and carried the glass to Victor. He appeared to be sleeping.

"Sweetheart?" she whispered.

His eyes opened. He blinked. Her gown was satin with tulle frill and crystals sewn into the fabric.

"Look at you . . . So beautiful."

She bit her lower lip. How long had it been since he'd complimented her looks? In the early years, he used to do it often, whispering to her at country club dances, "How's it feel to be the best-looking woman in the room?"

"I don't want to go. Listen to your voice—"

"Go. Nothing's going to happen in one night."

"You promise?"

"Go and come back."

"I brought you some tea."

"Thank you."

"Make sure he drinks it," she said to Roger, who sat dutifully in the corner of the living room. Roger nodded. She turned back to her husband.

"Do you like these earrings? You gave me them on our thirtieth, remember?"

"Yes."

"I always loved these."

"They look terrific."

"I'll see you in a few hours."

"All right."

"I'll be as quick as I can."

"I'll be . . ."

His voice trailed off.

"What, sweetheart?"

"Here. I'll be here."

"Good."

She kissed him on the forehead and patted his chest. Then she quickly rose, hiding her tears, and walked away. Her heels clicked on the hallway tile until the sound faded.

Victor felt torn and guilty.

His final sentence to Grace had been a lie. He would not be here when she returned. He would leave while she was gone, and be on his way to the cryonics facility. That was the plan, the reason he'd encouraged her to attend the gala.

He nearly called her back. But a wave of dizziness came over him, his head drooped, and he rolled to the side. Everything he had planned for, all these weeks and months, really all his adult life, was to culminate in the next few hours. It was no time to deviate. Stick to the plan.

Still . . .

He called for Roger, who approached, and he whispered something to his lowered ear.

"Do you understand?" Victor gasped. "No hesitation if that happens?"

"I understand," Roger said.

Victor inhaled weakly. "Let's go, then."

It was 8 P.M. Lorraine dressed in front of the mirror.

She hated New Year's parties. But she went to one every year. Her divorced friends had made a pact not to leave each other alone on nights when loneliness had extra strength.

She sprayed her hair. She peeked down the hall to see if Sarah had emerged. She was worried about her daughter, who had barely left her room in five days, wearing the same black sweatpants and old green T-shirt. She wanted to ask about whomever the high heels had been for, but she never got any traction with such subjects. Sarah would just freeze her out.

Lorraine remembered back when New Year's Eve was still a family thing, and the one December all three of them went into the city and stood shivering in Times Square, watching the ball drop. Sarah was seven years old, still small enough to sit on Tom's shoulders. She ate honey-roasted pecans they'd bought from a street cart, and it started snowing just before midnight. Sarah screamed, "three . . . two . . . one . . . Happy New Year!" along with a million other people.

Lorraine had been happy that night. She'd taken lots of pictures. But when they got in the car, Tom wiped the snow from his hair and said, "Well, we never have to do *that* again."

She went down the hall and knocked on Sarah's door.

She heard slow music playing. A female singer.
"Honey?"
It took a moment.

"What?" came the flat reply.

"Just saying bye."

"Bye."

"Happy New Year."

"Yep."

"I won't be back late."

"Bye."

Lorraine heard a car honking outside. Her friends.

"Do you have anyone to hang out with tonight?" She hated to even ask that question.

"I don't want to hang out, Mom."

"OK." She shook her head. "Tomorrow we'll have breakfast, all right?"

Silence.

"Sarah?"

"Not too early."

"Not too early," Lorraine said.

Another honk.

"I'll call you later, sweetie."

She headed downstairs. She sighed when she reached the door. She was glad she wasn't the designated driver this year. She really wanted a drink.

Sarah had already been drinking. A bottle of vodka she had taken from the dining room cabinet.

She would end her life tonight. It made the most sense. Her mother would be gone. The house was quiet. No chance of someone discovering her. Didn't people call New Year's the loneliest night on the calendar? She took comfort in knowing somewhere on the planet, someone might be as miserable as she was.

Don't they know it's the end of the world?
It ended when I lost your love.

She had downloaded that song after finding out the singer's name and had played it on her cell phone for days. She barely left her room. Didn't shower. Hardly ate. When her mother saw her emerge from the bathroom the day before, wearing the same black sweatpants and old green T-shirt, she asked, "What's going on with you, honey?" Sarah lied, said she was working on college stuff and letting herself be grubby.

She drank a swig now straight from the vodka bottle and felt it burn down her throat. *Maybe they'll ask Ethan about vodka when I'm dead,* she thought, *make him admit the girl he so wasn't interested in was drinking with him a couple of weeks ago.* She knew she could not face seeing him again, or anyone who knew him, or anyone who knew about the two of them, which was everyone now, wasn't it? There was no cover. No shelter. No hiding in class behind her lowered head and outstretched elbow. She knew how this went. Everyone talking about you. Smirking behind your back. Posting more and more comments. *"Seriously?" "Run, dude!" "Knew she was a skank."* God! The *glee* they took in ripping her, in joining Ethan's disbelief that loser Sarah Lemon should ever try to climb out of her hole. She felt worthless and hollow. There was no hope of fixing this.

And when hope is gone, time is punishment.

"End it now," she whispered.

She took the vodka and the phone and stumbled to the garage.

62

Father Time had been watching them both.

First he stood by Victor's dying body. He saw Roger load it into a van. He followed that van to the cryonics facility, where a warehouse garage door opened with a growl.

He saw the fourteenth-richest man in the world unloaded like a delivery and taken inside.

It was an hour before midnight on the last night of the year. Roger and Jed lowered the side rails of Victor's bed. A doctor and a coroner whispered to each other. They held documents. A huge tub was nearby, larger than a human body and filled with ice.

Victor was barely conscious, his breath coming in short spurts. The doctor asked if he wanted a sedative, but he shook his head.

"Is the paperwork right?" he mumbled.

The coroner told him yes, and Victor inhaled deeply and shut his eyes. The last thing he was aware of was Jed, the cryonics man, removing a pocket watch from his grip and saying, "I promise to take care of this."

Four hands went under his body, to lift him up.

But Dor was standing in the corner.

He turned his hourglass.

Meanwhile, in a garage in the suburbs, Sarah Lemon had turned the key in the ignition of the blue Ford Taurus.

Now all she had to do was wait. The fumes would take care of the rest. So easy. She deserved something easy. She took a gulp from the vodka bottle and spit some down her chin and shirt. Through her cell phone the sad song played again and again, barely audible over the engine noise.

I wake up in the morning and I wonder
Why everything's the same as it was
I can't understand, no I can't understand
How life goes on the way it does.

"Leave me alone," Sarah murmured, picturing Ethan and his cocky posture and his thick hair and the way he walked. He'd be sorry, she told herself. He'd feel guilty.

Why does my heart go on beating?

She was terribly woozy.

Why do these eyes of mine cry?

She slumped backward.

Don't they know

She coughed.

it's the end of the world?

She coughed again.

It ended when you said good-bye.

Her eyes began to close. Then everything seemed to stop. Through the windshield, she thought she saw a man moving closer. She thought she heard him scream.

63

Dor screamed in frustration.

Having turned the hourglass, what else was he to do? He could slow time, but never stop it completely. The cars he'd examined had always been moving, just at infinitesimal speed. The people he'd studied still breathed, just so slowly they would never know he was there.

The power of the hourglass had let him bend and squeeze the moments around him—a power beyond comprehension when granted—but Dor realized it was not enough. Eventually, time would pass. Eventually, Victor would be covered in ice and cut open. Eventually, carbon monoxide would spread through Sarah's bloodstream, cause hypoxia, a poisoned nervous system, heart failure.

This could not have been why he was sent to Earth—to watch them die. They were Dor's mission, his destiny. Yet both had taken extreme measures before he could affect anything. He had failed. It was too late.

Unless . . .

It is never too late or too soon, the old man had said. *It is when it is supposed to be.*

Dor crouched in front of two garbage cans. He put his hands together, pressed them to his lips, and shut his eyes, the way he used to do in the cave, trying to isolate the voice within from the millions of voices outside.

It is when it is supposed to be.

This moment? But then, how did he *stay* in this moment? Dor thought back on all that he understood about time.

What was the constant?

Movement. Yes. With time there was always *movement.* The setting sun. The dripping water. The pendulums. The spilling sand. To realize his destiny, such movement had to cease. He had to stop the flow of time *completely* . . .

His eyes opened. He quickly rose. He reached inside the car, and lifted Sarah by her knees and shoulders.

The old year was nearly over. A new year was minutes away. Father Time carried the dying girl out into the snow; you could count the flakes hanging in the moonlight.

He walked through a winter landscape of traffic and party lights.

He walked with Sarah's head rolled into his chest, her eyes half-opened, looking up at him. He felt sorry for this girl. *One who wants too little time.* That's how the old man had described her.

Dor thought about his own children. He wondered if they'd ever become this unhappy, wanting to give up on the world. He hoped not. But then, hadn't he wished his own life would end many times?

He walked along an expressway and through a tunnel and past a crowded stadium parking lot whose sign read NEW YEAR'S HIP-HOP ALL NIGHT CELEBRATION. He walked for two days on his clock, barely a second on ours, until he reached a darkened industrial park and the cryonics building.

He had to bring Sarah and Victor together. If this moment was *when it is supposed to be,* then Dor could no longer traverse two existences.

He carried Sarah to the warehouse with the large storage cylinders inside. He rested her against a wall. Then he went to the room where Victor was being prepped. He lifted Victor's body from the bed surrounded by others, and brought him to the warehouse, too, placing him next to Sarah. He put a thumb to each of their wrists, and eventually felt the slowest bump of a pulse. They were suspended, but still alive.

That meant Dor's idea had a chance.

He crouched between them and pulled their hands to the hourglass.

He wrapped their fingers around the braided posts, hoping this would connect them to the source of its power. Then he stretched his own hand over the top, gripped hard, and turned.

The top came loose. He pulled it away. It floated into the air, casting a blue light over the three of them. Looking into the upper bulb, Dor saw the white sand exposed, so fine and sparkly it refracted like diamonds.

Herein lies every moment of the universe.

Dor hesitated. Either he was right, and his story had a yet untold ending, or he was wrong and his story was over.

He placed his thumb and forefinger close together, and, whispering the word "Alli"—should he perish, he wanted that to be the last thing he said—he pushed into the sand, toward the narrow funnel that separated what had fallen from what had not.

Instantly, his mind went dizzy with a billion images. His fingers tingled as the flesh melted off the bones, and they elongated into stick-like digits, growing thin as pins until they slid through the hourglass stem. Every instant of the universe was passing through Dor's consciousness; his mind was traveling through that glass as well, traversing what had already transpired and what was yet to be.

Finally, with a power that did not come from man, he pinched his pin-like fingertips together. His eyes seemed to explode in color. His head was thrown back.

He had plucked a single falling grain of sand, just as it was about to hit bottom.

And this is what happened next . . .

On seashores from Los Angeles to Tripoli, ocean waves froze in mid-curl.

Clouds stopped moving. Weather locked. Raindrops in Mexico hung in the air, and a sandstorm in Tunisia became a permanent grainy billow.

There was not a sound on Earth. Airplanes hung silently above runways. Puffs of cigarette smoke remained solid around their smokers. Phones were dead. Screens were blank. No one spoke. No one breathed. Sunlight and darkness divided the planet, and New Year's fireworks remained splattered in nighttime skies, drizzled purples and greens, as if children had been drawing on the firmament then had run away.

No one was born. No one died. Nothing drew closer. Nothing went away. The proverbial march of time had gone to its knees.

One man.

One grain of sand.

Father Time had stopped the world.

STILLNESS

⊰ 64 ⊱

Victor had expected more pain.

Beyond the cancer, beyond his rotting liver, the shock of a sudden body freeze would be, he imagined, traumatic. He'd once had a bucket of ice water dumped on his head at a sporting event—part of a celebration—and his nerve endings felt as if they'd been raked with knives. He could only imagine the effect of full ice immersion. When he'd closed his eyes in the cryonics facility, he'd braced for that.

Instead, there was a sudden lightness to him, and a freedom of movement he had long ago forgotten. He gripped one side of the bed—only he saw now that it was not the bed he was gripping but an . . . *hourglass* of some kind, and he was in the warehouse with the huge fiberglass cylinders and . . . what happened?

He stood up.

No pain.

No wheelchair.

"Who are *you*?" a girl's voice asked.

65

Sarah had thought she was gripping the steering wheel.

But as her vision cleared, she saw her hand was on the post of a strange-looking hourglass. A dream, she figured. It had to be. A room she'd never seen before? Some old guy in a bathrobe, asleep on the floor? She felt OK, not even dizzy from the alcohol, so she stood up and looked around, free and light, the way you feel in dreams when your feet don't touch the ground.

Wait . . .

She stomped her feet. She did not feel the ground.

Wait . . .

Where did the garage go? The car? That song? She suddenly remembered the darkness that had strangled her, so thoroughly she wanted to die. But had she? Where *was she*?

She moved out of the warehouse, down a hallway to a smaller room. She looked inside and recoiled. She thought she saw four men around a big tub—only they weren't moving. There was no sound. Suddenly this felt like one of those zombie dreams, and she hurried back to the big room where she'd awakened, only to see the old guy was up and moving around.

"Who are *you*?" she screamed.

He glared at her.

"Who are *you*?" he snapped back. "How did you get in here?"

She hadn't expected a response—certainly not a scolding one. She felt suddenly terrified. What if this wasn't a dream? *What had she done?* She saw a single open door near the loading area, and she ran through it into the snowy night. A car down the street had its lights on but was not moving. A gas station seemed open, but a customer held the hose in his arms, like a guard on sentry duty. Strangest of all, the snowflakes were stuck in the sky. When Sarah swatted at them, her hand passed through.

She dropped to the ground and curled her body into a ball, covering her eyes, squeezing them shut, trying to understand if she was dead or alive.

66

Victor wondered if he was between worlds.

He had heard tales of people who floated in near-death experiences. Perhaps it happened when you were frozen alive. Your body locked, but your soul was left to wander. No wheelchairs? No canes? It was not the worst thing to be free of flesh and bones until science beckoned for your second act.

Only two things bothered him.

He was still inside his body.

And what about the girl?

She'd worn a green T-shirt and black sweatpants and was not at all familiar. A loose, random thought? he wondered. One of those faces that appears in a dream but you just can't identify?

Anyhow, she was gone now. He moved past the giant storage tanks of liquid nitrogen and wondered if he hadn't, in another dimension, already been placed inside one. Maybe that was it. His body inside, his soul outside? How might time be moving elsewhere when it wasn't moving here?

He tried to touch the cylinders, but made no contact. He tried to grab a ladder, but his palms could not grip the sides. In fact, he could not feel anything he saw. It was like trying to feel your reflection in the mirror.

"What is this place?"

He spun around. The girl had returned. She was holding her elbows as if she were cold.

"Why am I here?" She was trembling. "Who *are* you?"

Now Victor was lost. If his soul were projecting, there would be no explanation for this, another person equally conscious and in the same space, asking questions.

Unless . . .

Her body was inside the tanks? She, too, was being frozen?

"What is this place?" she repeated.

"You don't know?"

"I've never seen it before."

"It's a laboratory."

"For what?"

"Storing people."

"Storing . . . ?"

"Freezing them."

Her eyes widened and she stepped back. "I don't want . . . I don't want . . ."

"Not you," he concluded.

He walked to a cylinder and again tried to touch it. Nothing. He saw the flowers in the numbered white boxes and tried to kick them, but could not displace a petal.

It made no sense now. His body? This girl? All his carefully controlled plans? He turned his back and slid down, sitting on the floor but feeling no floor beneath him.

"Are people *inside* those things?" she asked.

"Yes."

"And you were supposed to be?"

He looked away.

She sat down, too, a respectful distance away.

"God . . . ," she whispered. "Why?"

Victor, over the years, rarely spoke about his life to strangers.

He almost never gave interviews, believing that, in finance, secrecy was an ally. Information might be inadvertently shared, and the next day a rival would beat you to the punch. The quick and the dead. That was the joke about life forms in the business world. *Only two kinds. The quick and the dead.*

Now Victor Delamonte was neither.

This setting—this nothingness in the cryonics facility—was either purgatory or a hallucination. Whatever the case, Victor had no more use for secrets. So he told a girl in sweatpants what he had told almost no one else, about his cancer, about the kidney disease and the dialysis, about his plan to outmaneuver death with a second lifetime deep in the future.

He told her he should not be here, in this warehouse. He told her he was supposed to awaken many years from now, as a fully living medical miracle, not some ghost.

She listened to his story. She even nodded at some scientific references, which surprised him. This girl was smarter than she looked—considering she looked as if she'd slept on a park bench. He stopped before admitting he was seconds away from ice immersion in the other room. It seemed like too much.

At one point, the girl asked how his wife felt about him freezing himself.

Victor hesitated.

"Oh," she said. "You didn't tell her."

Smarter than she looked.

Sarah Lemon used to talk with her parents.

Listening to Victor reminded her of that. As a child she would sit on the floor of their bedroom, twirling the frills on a throw pillow and answering their questions about school. She was a straight-A student, gifted at math and science, and her father, Tom, a lab technician, would stand at the mirror, run a hand through his thinning blond hair, and tell her to keep it up; if she wanted to be a doctor, he expected nothing less. Lorraine, who sold radio advertising, would lean back in the bed, drag on a cigarette, and say, "I'm proud of you, sweetie. Run and get me one of those ice cream bars, will you?"

"You don't need another ice cream bar," Tom would say.

They divorced when Sarah was twelve. Lorraine got the house, the furniture, all the ice cream bars she wanted, and full-time custody of their only child. Tom got a hair transplant, a boat, and a young female friend named Melissa, who had no interest in spending time with someone else's daughter. They married and moved to Ohio.

Publicly, Sarah took her mother's side, said she was happy to be staying with "the good parent," the one who hadn't messed things up. But deep down, like many children, she missed the absent party and wondered how much she was to blame for the marriage's collapse. The less her father called, the more she ached for him; the more her mother hugged her, the less she wanted the embrace. She looked like her mother and she sounded like her mother, and by eighth grade, she began to feel like her mother, unloved or perhaps unlovable. She ate too much and she put on weight, and she distanced herself from other kids and stayed inside studying because her father had admired that and maybe deep down she thought it would bring them closer. She sent him her grades every semester. Sometimes he responded with a note. *"Good girl, Sarah. Keep it up."* Sometimes he didn't.

By high school, her friends were few and her routine was predictable: science labs, bookstore browsing, weekends at home on the computer, parties something she heard about—past tense—during Monday morning homerooms when other kids were bragging. She'd been approached by a few boys from her math classes and she'd gone out with a couple of them—to movies, a school dance, video arcades—even made out a few times to see what everyone was talking about, but those boys eventually stopped calling and she was privately relieved. She never felt the slightest spark and figured she never would.

Ethan changed all that. He put an end to her deadening drift. The thought of his face replaced all her other thoughts. She would drop the world for Ethan. She had.

But he had never really wanted her. And in the end, he exposed her for what she'd always feared she was: pathetic. After that, there was no bottom to the pit.

She told most of this to Victor, the old man in the bathrobe, after he had told her his story about the freezing thing and his wife. They were alone in this eerie warehouse, and Sarah felt so frazzled and confused and she figured maybe he knew more than he let on. But the further she got into the Ethan story, the more she felt the old soak of depression. She stopped just before the final moments in the garage, with the vodka and the sad song and the engine running. She wasn't going to admit she had tried to kill herself. Not to a total stranger.

When he asked how she had gotten to this facility, she said she didn't know—and she truly did not—she'd just woken up holding an hourglass.

"I kind of remember being carried."

"Carried?"

"By this guy."

"What guy?"

"He works in a clock shop."

Victor looked at her as if she'd just been painted pink.

From behind a cylinder, they heard a noise.

69

Dor coughed.

His eyes opened, as if coming out of sleep, although he hadn't slept in thousands of years. He was lying on the floor, and he blinked several times before he realized that Victor and Sarah were standing over him.

They immediately peppered him with questions—"Who are you?" "Where are we?"—as Dor tried to clear his head. He remembered only the screaming colors and everything going black and a sensation of him falling through the air and the hourglass—*where was the hourglass?*—and then he saw it in Sarah's grip, the top reattached, and he realized that if they were alive, he had guessed correctly. Now he could—

Wait.

Had he coughed?

"What do you have to do with all this?" Victor asked.

"How did I get here?" Sarah said.

"Was I drugged?"

"Where's my house?"

"Why do I feel healthy?"

"Where's the car?"

Dor could not focus. He had *coughed*. In his eternity in the cave, he had never coughed, sneezed, or even breathed hard.

"Talk to us," Victor said.

"Talk to us," Sarah said.

Dor looked down at his right hand. The flesh had returned to his fingers. His fist was clenched shut. He uncurled it.

A single grain of sand.

On the wall of his cave, Dor once carved the shape of a rolling pin.

It symbolized the delivery of their first child. A difficult pregnancy in Dor's time required midwives to soothe the belly with oils or a special rolling pin. Dor watched as they did this over Alli's womb, and Alli cried out as they prayed for her. The baby came, healthy, and Dor often wondered how such a simple thing—a rolling pin, found in even the poorest dwellings— could affect such a monumental event.

The answer, he was later told by an Asu, was that only a magical rolling pin could do it. Magic came from the gods. And when the gods touched something, the normal became the supernatural, the simple became the wondrous.

A rolling pin to bring forth a child.

A grain of sand to stop the world.

Now Dor looked at a young girl in sweatpants, and an old man in his bathrobe, and he realized the magic of the elements had brought him this far.

What remained would be up to him.

"Just tell us," Sarah said, her voice starting to quiver. "Are we . . . dead?"

Dor struggled to his feet.

"No," he said.

For the first time in six thousand years, he felt tired.

"You have not died," he began. "You are in the middle of a moment."

He held out the grain of sand. "This moment."

"What are you talking about?" Victor asked.

"The world has been stopped. Your lives are stopped in it—although your souls are here now. What you have done to this point cannot be undone. What you do next . . ."

He hesitated.

"What?" Victor said. *"What?"*

"It is still unwritten."

Sarah looked to Victor, who looked back. Both of them were picturing their last remembered moment: Sarah slumped in the car, inhaling poison; Victor lifted toward the ice, about to become a medical experiment.

"How did I get here?" Sarah asked.

"I carried you," Dor said.

"What do we do now?" Victor asked.

"There is a plan."

"What is it?"

"That is yet unknown to me."

"How can there be a plan if you don't know what it is?"

Dor rubbed his forehead several times. He winced.

"Are you OK?" Sarah asked.

"Pain."

"I don't get it. Why us?"

"Your fates matter."

"More than the rest of the world?"

"Not more."

"How did you even find us?"

"I heard your voices."

"Stop!" Victor raised his palms. "Stop this. Enough. Voices? Fates? You're a repair guy in a clock shop."

Dor shook his head. "In this moment, it is not wise to judge with your eyes."

Victor looked away, attempting, as he always did, to solve things himself when others were incompetent. Dor lifted his chin. He opened his mouth. His vocal cords became those of a nine-year-old French boy.

"Make it yesterday."

Victor spun, recognizing the sound of himself. Now the voice became Victor's deeper adult version. *"Another lifetime."* Dor turned to Sarah. *"Make it stop,"* he said, sounding just like her.

Sarah and Victor stared in stunned silence. How could this man know their private thoughts?

"Before I came to you," he said, "you came to me."

Sarah studied his face.

"You don't really fix clocks, do you?"

"I prefer them broken."

"Why is that?" Victor said.

Dor looked at the grain of sand in his fingers.

"Because I am the sinner who created them."

FUTURE

70

In Dor's happier days on Earth, his son once asked him an unusual question.

"Who will I marry?"

Dor smiled and said he didn't know.

"But you said the stones can tell you what will happen."

"The stones can tell me many things," Dor said. "They can tell me when the sun will come, when it will set, how many nights until the moon is as full as your round face."

He squeezed his son's cheeks. The boy laughed then looked away.

"But those are hard things," he said.

"Hard?"

"The sun and the moon. They are far away. I only want to know who I will marry. If you can tell the hard things, why can't you tell me that?"

Dor smiled to himself. His son was asking the kind of questions he had asked as a boy. And Dor remembered his own frustration when he could not get an answer.

"Why do you want to know?"

"Well," the boy said, "if those stones said I will marry Iltani, I would be happy."

Dor nodded. Iltani was the shy, pretty daughter of a brick maker. She might indeed grow to be a fetching bride.

"What if the stones said you will marry Gildesh?"

His son made a face, as Dor had known he would.

"Gildesh is too big and too loud!" the boy protested. "If the stones said I would marry her, I would run away now!"

Dor laughed and tousled his son's hair. The boy picked up one of the stones and threw it.

"No, Gildesh!" he yelled.

Dor watched it fly across the yard.

Now Dor looked at Sarah, remembering that moment.

He wondered what became of young Gildesh—was she rejected by men as this Sarah had been? He thought about his son's stone flying across the yard, the youthful idea that you could toss away the future if you didn't like it—and he realized, suddenly, what he needed to do.

He held up the hourglass, looked inside, and saw, as he had suspected, that the sand in the top remained in the top, and the sand in the bottom remained in the bottom. Nothing passed between. Time was not advancing.

Dor squeezed the top panel and once again removed it from the ancient timepiece.

"What are you doing?" Victor asked.

"What I have been commanded to do," Dor said.

He poured out, across the warehouse floor, the sand from the upper bulb—the sand of what was yet to happen—and it kept pouring and pouring, more sand than seemed possible from a hundred hourglasses, let alone one. Then he laid the timepiece on its side, and it enlarged to the size of a giant tunnel, the path of sand leading into its center, shimmering the way moonlight shimmers on the ocean.

Removing his shoes, Dor stepped into the sand. He motioned to Sarah and Victor.

"Come," he said.

He looked at his arms. For the first time in six thousand years, he was sweating.

Einstein once postulated that if you traveled at an enormous rate of speed, time would actually slow down relative to the world you left behind,

so that seeing the future without aging alongside it was, at least theoretically, possible.

Sarah had studied this in physics class. So had Victor, decades earlier. Now, in the frozen space between a single breath, they were being asked to test the theory, to move forward while the world stood still, to walk along sand into a giant hourglass at the behest of a lean, dark-haired man in a black turtleneck who—as far as they knew—worked in a clock shop.

"Are you going?" Sarah said, turning to Victor.

"I don't buy any of this," he answered. "I had paperwork. Contracts. Someone is deliberately sabotaging my plans."

Sarah swallowed. For some reason, she really wanted this old guy to come with her, if only so she wouldn't be alone. He felt like the most important friend she could have.

"Please?" she asked, softly.

Victor looked away. Every logical bone told him no. He didn't know this girl. And this clock shop guy could be anybody, any charlatan, any hocus-pocus fake. But the way she said it. *Please.* Silly as it seemed, it was the purest word he had heard in months. Few people ever got close enough to Victor to ask things in a personal way.

He glanced around the cryonics facility. All that waited here was a frozen, untouchable panorama. He looked at Sarah.

When we are most alone is when we embrace another's loneliness.

Victor took her hand.

Everything went black.

71

At first, it felt like climbing an invisible bridge.

They proceeded up through a deep, lightless void, seeing nothing but each sandy footprint they made drifting away behind them, glowing gold before disappearing in the blackness.

Sarah squeezed Victor's hand.

"Are you all right?" he asked.

She nodded, yet gripped him harder as they descended. She was trembling, as if some awful fate awaited her. Sarah was not like him, Victor thought. He was anxious to see how his second life would play out. But something terrible had happened to this girl. No matter how smart she appeared, she was fragile at her core.

They lowered into a mist. When it lifted, they were inside a warehouse, with food and beverages stacked on the shelves.

"What is this?" Victor asked Dor. "Where are we?"

Dor said nothing. But Sarah recognized the place immediately. It was the site of her fateful date with Ethan. *"Over at my uncle's if u want 2 come."* She had replayed that night so many times—the kissing, the drinking, the way it ended. And suddenly, there he was again, the boy of her dreams, in his familiar jeans and hooded sweatshirt, walking toward them. Sarah drew in a breath. But he passed without a glance.

"He can't see us?" Victor asked.

"We are not in this time," Dor said. "These are the days to come."

"The future?"

"Yes."

Victor noticed Sarah's expression.

"This is the guy?" he asked.

Sarah nodded. She felt pangs of heartbreak just seeing him again. If this were the future, did that mean she was gone? And if she were gone, did Ethan regret what he had done? He was alone. He was tapping on his phone. Perhaps he was thinking about her. Perhaps that's why he'd come to the warehouse. Perhaps he was mourning her, looking at her photo, the way she so often had looked at his. She started to move toward him, when he smiled and lifted a thumb and said "Hah!" A beeping sound indicated he was playing a video game.

A sudden knock drew his attention. He opened the warehouse door, and a girl about Sarah's age entered, her hair blown out and styled, her hands dug in her coat pockets. Sarah noticed her plentiful makeup.

"Hey, what's up?" Ethan said.

Sarah winced. *Those words.*

She listened to them talk. She heard the girl say it was unfair, the way people were blaming him.

"I know, right?" Ethan said. "I didn't do anything. It was *her* fault. The whole thing is out of control."

The girl took off her coat and asked if it was all right to eat something from the shelves. Ethan grabbed two boxes of crackers. He also pulled down a vodka bottle.

"Can't lose with booze," he said.

Sarah felt suddenly weak, as if she'd been kicked in the knees. Her final thought as she'd sunk into death was that Ethan would be sorry, that his inner torture would somehow equal hers. But hurting ourselves to inflict pain on others is just another cry to be loved. And that cry, Sarah now realized, seeing Ethan grab two paper cups, had been as unheard as the feelings she once declared for him in a parking lot.

Her death was as insignificant as her life.

She looked pleadingly at Dor.

"Why did you bring me here?" she said.

The walls seemed to melt and the setting changed. They were now at the shelter where Sarah worked on Saturdays. Homeless men lined up for breakfast.

An older woman was scooping oatmeal. A man in a blue cap stepped forward.

"Where's Sarah?" he asked.

"She's not here today," the woman said.

"Sarah puts in extra bananas."

"OK. Here's some extra bananas."

"I like that girl. She's quiet, but I like her."

"We haven't heard from her in a couple of weeks."

"I hope she's all right."

"Me, too."

"I'll be praying for her then."

Sarah blinked. She didn't think anyone there knew her name. She certainly didn't think they'd miss her if she weren't around. *I like that girl. She's quiet, but I like her.*

Sarah watched the man sit alongside other homeless clients. Despite their awful circumstances, they were going on with life, getting through it as best they could. Sarah wondered how she could have ignored this every Saturday while being so dazzled by a boy. The man who liked bananas thought more about her than Ethan did.

The shame welled up inside her.

She turned to Dor.

She swallowed hard.

"Where's my mom?" she whispered.

Once more, the scene changed. It was daytime, and snow was piled against the curbs.

Sarah, Dor, and Victor were in the parking lot of a car dealership. A salesman emerged from the office, wearing a winter parka and holding a clipboard. He walked right through them and approached the passenger side of a gray van.

Lorraine sat inside.

"It's freezing," the man said through the window, his breath condensing in smoke. "You sure you don't want to come in?"

Lorraine shook her head and quickly signed the papers. Sarah moved toward her cautiously.

"Mom?" she whispered.

The salesman took the paperwork. Lorraine watched him go. She squeezed her lips tightly as tears slid down her cheeks. Sarah remembered all the times she had cried just that way in her mother's arms, over teasing in school, over the divorce. Her mother, crazy as she sometimes was, had always had time for her, always stroked her hair and told her things would be all right.

Now Sarah was helpless to do the same.

She saw another man approach the car, folding papers into an envelope. Her Uncle Mark, from North Carolina. He got into the driver's seat.

"Well, that's it," he said. "Sorry you even had to come, but they wouldn't take it if you didn't sign."

Lorraine exhaled weakly. "I never want to see that car again."

"Yeah," he said.

They watched silently as the salesman drove the blue Ford toward the rear of the lot.

"Let's get going," Mark said.

"Wait."

Lorraine kept her eyes locked on the car, until it disappeared around a corner. Then she broke down, sobbing.

"I should have been there, Mark."

"It's not your fault—"

"I'm her *mother*!"

"It's not your fault."

"Why would she do this? *Why didn't I know?*"

He tried awkwardly to hug her across the front seat, their winter coats scratching against each other.

Sarah gripped her elbows. She felt sick inside. She had been so consumed with escaping her own misery, she hadn't considered the misery she might inflict. She saw her mother squeeze the envelope to her chest, clinging to the receipt for a car Sarah had used to kill herself, because it was the last thing she had of her daughter.

Dor stepped in front of Sarah. He softly repeated the question Lorraine had asked.

"Why?"

Why?

Why take her own life? Why die in a garage? Why cause this pain to anyone she loved?

Sarah wanted to explain it all, the humiliation of Ethan's rejection, the shameful feeling caused by his friends, the shock of seeing your secrets exposed through a computer screen, your future shattering so completely in front of you that dying with a lungful of poison seems like a relief.

She wanted to blame him, to blame her whole rotten existence. But seeing Ethan, seeing her mother, seeing the world after the world she had known, somehow took her to the very bottom, the end of self-delusion, and the truth enveloped her like a cocoon, and all she said was, "I was so *lonely*."

And Father Time said, "You were never alone."

With that, he put his hand over Sarah's eyes.

What she saw, suddenly, was a cave, and a bearded man with his face in his palms. His eyes were squeezed shut.

"That's you?" she whispered.

"Away from the one I love."

"For how long?"

"As long as time itself."

She saw him rise to the cave wall and carve a symbol. Three wavy lines.

"What's that?"

"Her hair."

"Why are you drawing it?"

"To remember."

"She died?"

"I wanted to perish, too."

"You really loved her?"

"I would have given my life."

"Would you have taken it?"

"No, child," he said. "That is not ours to do."

Dor realized, in uttering those words, that he may have been kept alive all these millenniums just for this moment. Living without love was something he knew more about than any soul on Earth. The more Sarah spoke of loneliness, the clearer it became why he was there.

"I made such a fool of myself," she lamented.

"Love does not make you a fool."

"He didn't love me back."

"That does not make you a fool, either."

"Just tell me . . ." Her voice cracked. "When does it stop hurting?"

"Sometimes never."

Sarah saw the bearded Dor alone in the cave.

"How did you survive?" she asked. "All that time with your wife not with you?"

"She was always with me," he said.

Dor removed his hand from Sarah's eyes. They watched the van drive down the snowy street.

"You had many more years," he said.

"I didn't want them."

"But they wanted you. Time is not something you give back. The very next moment may be an answer to your prayer. To deny that is to deny the most important part of the future."

"What's that?"

"Hope."

The shame welled up inside her, and once again, she wept. She missed her mother more than ever.

"I'm so sorry," Sarah gasped, tears pouring down her cheeks. "It just felt like . . . the end."

"Ends are for yesterdays, not tomorrows."

Dor waved a hand, and the street dissolved into sand. The skies turned a midnight purple, filled with countless stars.

"There is more for you to do in this life, Sarah Lemon."

"Really?" she whispered.

"Do you want to see?"

She thought for a moment, then shook her head.

"Not yet."

And Dor knew she was starting to heal.

72

All this time, Victor was watching.

He now understood the girl's shaky composure, her trembling shoulders, her fragile voice. She had tried to kill herself over a boy (he looked like a punk, Victor told himself, but then, he was biased; he was coming to like this Sarah). And she had been shown, in the end, what Victor would have told her a long time ago: No love is worth that trouble. He doubted Grace would end her life over him, no matter what he had done; and much as he deep down loved her, he was looking for a way to live beyond death, even if she didn't come with him.

What he still could not reason was how these hallucinations were being formed and who this clock shop man really was. Victor had noticed a change in him since they'd first met. Behind the store counter, he'd seemed solid, healthy, almost indestructible, but now he looked pale, he was perspiring, and his cough was growing worse. Victor, conversely, had never felt better—which was why he was certain this whole thing was some figment of his wandering brain. One did not simply wake up healthy and start floating through time.

He watched Dor, who was bent over in the sand, moving his fingers through it. Finally, he looked up at Victor. "There is something I must show you, too."

Victor recoiled. He was not interested in seeing the world he'd left behind.

"My story's different," Victor said.

"Come."

"You know I have a plan, right?"

Dor rose without a word, then wiped the sweat from his forehead and looked at his hand as if confused. He resumed his slow pace on the path, which tilted upward like the side of a hill. Victor turned to Sarah, who was still in the stunned throes of seeing her life revealed. Now it was Victor who wanted company.

"Are you coming?" he asked.

She stepped in behind him. They began to ascend.

73

This time, when the mist cleared, they were back in the cry-onics warehouse.

The huge fiberglass cylinders stood like monuments. One of them was slightly smaller and newer than the others.

"What are we seeing?" Victor asked. "Is this the future?"

Before Dor could answer, the door opened and Jed entered. He was followed by Grace, wearing a brown winter coat. She moved cautiously, looking around with every step.

"Is that your wife?" Sarah whispered.

Victor swallowed. He knew Grace would learn of his plan. He never imagined he'd watch her do it.

He saw Jed point out the smaller cylinder. He saw Grace draw her hands together over her mouth. He couldn't tell if she was praying or hiding her disgust.

"In that thing?" she said.

"He insisted on his own." Jed scratched his ear. "I'm sorry. I had no idea he didn't tell you."

Grace held her arms, uncertain whether she should approach the cylinder or move away from it.

"Can you see inside?"

"I'm afraid not."

"But his corpse is in there?"

"Patient."

"What?"

"We say 'patient.' Not 'corpse.'"

"What?"

"Forgive me. I know this must be hard."

They stood together in awkward silence, amid the low humming of electrical current. Finally, Jed cleared his throat and said, "Well . . . I'll leave you alone. You're welcome to sit."

He pointed to the mustard couch. Victor shook his head as if to stop him. He felt suddenly embarrassed, not only by the manipulation of his death, but by the ratty condolence chair his wife was being offered.

Grace did not sit down.

She thanked Jed and watched him go. Then she slowly approached the cylinder and let her fingers skim across the fiberglass exterior.

Her lower lip fell. She exhaled so hard, her shoulders drooped forward and she seemed to drop a couple of inches.

"Grace, it's OK," Victor blurted out. "It's—"

She whacked the cylinder with her fist.

She whacked it again.

Then she kicked it so hard she nearly fell backward.

When she straightened up, she sniffed once and walked to the exit, passing the mustard couch without so much as a glance.

The door closed. The silence seemed directed toward Victor personally. Dor and Sarah looked at him, but he looked away, feeling exposed. In his race to cheat death, he'd trusted scientists more than his wife. He had denied her their final intimacy. He had not even left a body to bury. How would she grieve him now? He doubted she would ever come to this place again.

He glanced at Sarah, who looked down, as if embarrassed.

He turned to Dor.

"Just show me," Victor growled, "if it worked."

74

Crowded. Incredibly crowded.

That was Victor's first impression of his future. They had followed the sand through the giant glass and descended from the void into another clearing mist, revealing massive high-rise buildings, packed thickly, block after block, in what Victor assumed to be a major metropolis centuries from now. There was almost no greenery and little color beyond steel blues and grays. The skies were dotted with unusual small aircraft, and the air itself had a different feel to it. It was thicker, dirtier, and cold as well, although the people did not dress for it. Their faces were different than those of his time, hair tints were like a paint-box assortment, heads seemed larger. It was difficult to tell men from women.

He saw no one old.

"Is this still Earth?" Sarah asked.

Dor nodded.

"Then I made it?" Victor said. "I'm alive?"

Dor nodded again. They were standing in the middle of a huge urban square, as tens of thousands of people scurried around them, heads down in devices or speaking into dark glasses that floated in front of their eyes.

"How far in the future is this?" Sarah said.

Victor surveyed the surroundings. "If I had to guess, a few hundred years."

He almost smiled.

Because he judged life by success and failure, Victor believed he had won.

He had eluded death and resurfaced in the future.

"So where am I in all this?" he asked.

Dor pointed and the vista changed. They were now inside a huge, open hall, lit from the sides, silver and white, with massive, high ceilings and screens that floated in midair.

Victor appeared on every one.

"What the hell is going on?" he asked. The screens were playing moments from Victor's life. He saw himself in his thirties, shaking hands in a boardroom, and in his fifties, delivering a keynote speech in London, and in his eighties, in the doctor's office with Grace, looking at CT scans. Clusters of people studied the screens as if this were an exhibition. Perhaps he'd become a legend in the future? Victor thought. A medical miracle? Who knows? Maybe he owned this building.

But where would they get such images? These moments had never been filmed. He saw a scene from a few weeks ago, Victor staring out the office window at a man sitting on a skyscraper.

"That was you, wasn't it?" he asked Dor.

"Yes."

"Why were you staring at me?"

"I was wondering why you wished to live beyond a lifetime."

"Why wouldn't I?"

"It is not a gift."

"And how would you know that?"

Dor wiped his brow.

"Because I have done it."

75

Before Victor could respond, a commotion rose from the gallery hall, now completely filled with spectators.

Sitting on floating chairs or crammed against the walls, they reacted loudly to what they were seeing.

On the screens were images of Victor's childhood in France; Victor bounced on his parents' laps, Victor fed by his grandmother with a soup spoon, Victor crying at his father's funeral and praying beside his mother. *Make it yesterday.* The crowd gave an audible gasp when he said that.

"Why are they watching my life?" Victor asked. "Where am I during all this?"

Dor pointed to a large glass tube in the corner of the facility.

"What's that?" Victor asked.

"Look and see," Dor said.

Victor approached it haltingly, easing through the crowd like an apparition. He reached the front and leaned into the glass.

A wave of horror engulfed him.

There, inside the tube, was a pinkish, shriveled version of his body, his muscles atrophied, his skin blotched as if burned, his head wired in multiple places, the wires running to numerous machines. His eyes were open and his lips were parted in a pained expression.

"This can't *be*." His voice rose. "I was supposed to be revived. I had papers. I paid good money!"

Victor recalled the lawyers' warning. *Can't protect against everything.* Had he foolishly ignored that in his rush to find an answer?

"What happened? Who's responsible for this?"

People kept moving through him, peering in at the naked body as if gazing into a fish tank.

Victor spun to Dor. "I had documents! Files!"

"Gone now," Dor said.

"I hired people to protect me."

"Gone now, too."

"What about my wealth?"

"Taken."

"There were laws!"

"There are new laws."

Victor slumped. Was this really how his grand plan turned out? Betrayal? Victimization? A futuristic freak show?

"What are they all doing?"

"Watching your memories."

"Why?"

"To remember how to feel."

Victor dropped to his knees.

He was so accustomed to being correct in his judgments. Had he been spared the smaller mistakes in life only to make the biggest one at the end?

He studied the faces watching his history. They seemed young, often beautiful, but blank.

"Everyone in this time can live longer than we imagined," Dor explained. "They fill every waking minute with action, but they are empty.

"To them, you are an artifact. And your memories are rare.

You are a reminder of a simpler, more satisfying world. One they no longer know."

Victor never would have thought of himself that way. Simple? Satisfying? Wasn't he always the hurried, insatiable one? But the time-hungry world had only accelerated since his freezing, and he realized that, relative to this future, Dor was right. The images on the screens all showed emotion. His boyhood tears when his sack of food was stolen. The shy smiles when meeting Grace in the company elevator. His longing gaze as she walked away on the last night of his life.

He watched that scene now, him in the bed, her in an evening gown, heading to the gala.

I'll be as quick as I can.

I'll be . . .

What, sweetheart?

Here. I'll be here.

He saw her disappear down the hall, believing she would see him again. Could he really have been that cruel? He suddenly missed her in the most powerful way. For the first time in his adult life, he wanted to go backward.

The screens showed Victor watching Grace leave. The crowd rose to its feet. The image switched to the inside of the glass tube, as a tear fell down the cheek of Victor's imprisoned body.

Victor felt one on his own cheek as well.

Dor reached over and took it on his finger.

"Do you understand now?" he asked. "With endless time, nothing is special. With no loss or sacrifice, we can't appreciate what we have."

He studied the teardrop. He thought back to the cave. And he knew, finally, why he had been chosen for this journey. He had lived an eternity. Victor wanted an eternity. It had taken Dor all these centuries to comprehend the last thing the old man had told him, the thing he shared with Victor now.

"There is a reason God limits our days."

"Why?"

"To make each one precious."

76

Only then did Father Time tell his story.

As his voice grew raspy and his cough more severe, he spoke to Victor and Sarah of the world into which he was born. He spoke of the sun stick he invented, and the water clock made of bowls, of his wife, Alli, and his three children, and the old man from Heaven who visited him as a child and would imprison him as an adult.

Most of the tale seemed implausible to his two listeners, although when Dor spoke about climbing Nim's tower, Sarah whispered, "Babel," and Victor mumbled, "That's just a myth."

When he reached the part about his time in the cave, Dor placed his hand over Victor's eyes and let him see the centuries of solitary confinement, the tortured loneliness of a world without the familiar—a wife, children, friends, a home. A second lifetime? A tenth? A thousandth? What did it matter? It was not his.

"I lived," Dor said, "but I was not alive."

Victor viewed Dor's attempted escapes, his pounding on the karst walls, his efforts to crawl into the glowing pool. He heard the cacophony of requests for time.

"What are all those voices?" he asked.

"Unhappiness," Dor said.

He explained how once we began to chime the hour, we lost the ability to be satisfied.

There was always a quest for more minutes, more hours, faster progress to accomplish more in each day. The simple joy of living between sunrises was gone.

"Everything man does today to be efficient, to fill the hour?" Dor said. "It does not satisfy. It only makes him hungry to do more. Man wants to own his existence. But no one owns time."

He lowered his hand from Victor's eyes. "When you are measuring life, you are not living it. I know."

He looked down. "I was the first to do it."

His face was even paler now. His hair was damp with sweat.

"How old are you?" Victor whispered.

Dor shook his head. The first man to count his days had no idea how many he had accumulated.

He took a deep, painful inhale.

And he collapsed.

77

Dor's lungs fought for air. His eyes rolled backward. He was stricken with an ancient plague.

For six thousand years, he had been granted immunity from the passing moments: the planet grew older; he never used a breath. But the equation had changed. He had stopped the world. And when the world no longer advanced, Father Time did. His skin blotched quickly. His decay was catching up.

"What's wrong with him?" Sarah asked.

"I don't know," Victor said. All around, the future was fading—the spectators, the room, the tube that contained his mortal shell, melting away like a photo in a fire. The hourglass shrunk down to its normal size, the sand gathering back into the upper bulb.

"We have to help him," Sarah said.

"How? You saw what he's been through. What do we know about helping him?"

You saw what he's been through.

"Wait," Sarah said. She lifted Dor's left arm to her face. "Take the other one," she told Victor.

They covered their eyes with his hands. And both of them saw the same moment: Dor leaning over his wife, her face perspiring, her skin blotched red as his was now. They saw him kissing her cheek, his tears mixing with hers.

I will stop your suffering. I will stop everything.

"Oh my God," Sarah whispered. "She had the same disease."

They saw Dor run to Nim's tower. They saw his desperate ascent. They saw what others in their time had dismissed as an impossible myth: the destruction of the tallest structure ever built by men.

And God's sole permitted survivor.

But when they saw Dor swept into the cave, saw him greeted by a robed old man who asked, *Is it power that you seek?*, both Victor and Sarah let go of his hands at the same time.

They looked at each other.

"You saw him, too?" Victor said.

Sarah nodded. "We have to take him back."

In their normal lives, they never would have met.

Sarah Lemon and Victor Delamonte were of two different worlds, one high school and fast food, the other boardrooms and white tablecloths.

But fates are connected in ways we don't understand. And at this moment, with the universe stopped, only the two of them could change the fate of the man who had tried to change theirs. Sarah held the hourglass as Victor removed the bottom. They did as they had seen Dor do, poured out the sand—this time from the lower bulb, the sand of the past—and spread it out as he had spread out the future.

When it was done, they reached beneath Dor's knees and shoulders.

"If this works," Sarah asked, "what happens to us?"

"I don't know," Victor said. He truly didn't. Dor had plucked them out from the world. Without him, there was no telling where their souls would drift.

"We'll stay together, right?" Sarah said.

"No matter what," Victor assured her.

They hoisted Father Time, stepped onto the path, and began moving forward.

There were no witnesses to what came next, and no telling how long it took.

But Victor and Sarah walked the sands of time gone by, their previously glowing footprints drifting up toward their feet.

As they descended, mists cleared. Skies lit with stars. Finally, amid hanging snowflakes and frozen traffic and people locked in celebration of a new year, one teenager and one old man stood beneath an awning at One Forty-Three Orchard.

They waited.

A door opened.

And a familiar-looking face, that of the proprietor, now dressed in the draped white robe he had worn in the cave, said in a soft voice, "Bring him here."

78

They stepped inside the clock shop and laid the body on the floor.

"Who is he?" Victor asked the old man.

"His name is Dor."

"He was sent here for us?"

"And for himself."

"Is he dying?"

"Yes."

"Are we dying?"

"Yes."

The old man saw the fear on their faces. His expression softened. "All who are born are always dying."

Victor looked at Dor, who was barely conscious, and realized he had been wrong about who he was, but he had been wrong about so many things, even about the pocket watch, which Dor had chosen not for its antique value but for the painted reminder of a family—father, mother, child—hoping Victor would realize what he had with Grace before it was too late.

"Why was he punished?" Victor asked.

"He was never punished."

"The cave? All those years?"

"That was a blessing."

"A blessing?"

"Yes. He learned to appreciate the life he had led."

"But it took so long," Sarah said.

The old man removed a ring from the throat of the hourglass.

"What is long?" he said.

He slipped the ring onto Dor's finger. A single grain of sand floated out of Dor's grip.

"What's going to happen to him?" Sarah asked.

"He will finish his story. As will you."

Dor was motionless, his eyes closed. His hands were limp on the floor.

"Is it too late?" Sarah whispered.

The old man took the empty hourglass and turned it upside down. He held the grain of sand above it.

"Never too late or too soon," he said.

And he let it go.

79

We do not realize the sound the world makes—unless, of course, it comes to a stop. Then, when it starts, it sounds like an orchestra.

Breaking waves. Whipping wind. Falling rain. Squawking birds. All throughout the universe, time resumed and nature sang.

Dor felt his head spin and his body drop. He awoke coughing in the dirt. A high, strong sun hung in the sky.

He knew immediately.

He was home.

He struggled to stand up. Ahead of him was Nim's tower, its top in the clouds. The path beneath his feet would take him to it.

He inhaled deeply, then turned the other way. With the chance to do what none in life ever get to do, he did not waver. He changed the history of his footsteps.

He ran back to her.

Through waves of heat and fits of choking, he pushed on, driven by desperation. Although the exertion would speed his death, he would not slow down. A phrase came to his memory—*time flies*—and he recited it over and over, driving him on through the hills and into the high plains. Only when the rocks looked familiar, only when he saw the hut made of reeds, did he slow his pace, as man does when he approaches what he desires, uncertain if it can possibly be all he hoped. Dare he look? All that he had dreamed of? All that had sustained him for an eternity?

His chest was heaving. He was drenched in sweat.

"Alli?" he cried.

He stepped around the hut.

She lay on a blanket.

"My love," she whispered.

Her voice was how he had always remembered it, and none of the billions of voices he had heard in that cave ever matched its sweetness or the way it made him feel.

"I am here," he said, kneeling down.

She saw his face.

"You are stricken."

"No more than you."

"Where did you go?"

He tried to answer, but he could no longer see his thoughts. Images were fading. An old man? A girl? He was back on his own path, and the memory of his eternal life was fading away.

"I tried to stop your suffering," he said.

"We cannot stop what Heaven chooses."

She smiled weakly.

"Stay with me."

"Forever."

He touched her hair. She turned her head.

"Look," she whispered.

The sky before them was painted by a stunning sunset, orange and violet and cranberry red. Dor lay down beside her. Their labored breathing overlapped. Once, Dor would have counted those breaths. Now he merely listened, absorbing the sound. He looked at everything. He took it all in. His hand drooped, and he found himself drawing a shape in the sand, wide at the top, narrow in the middle, wide at the bottom. What was it?

A wind blew, and the sand around his drawing scattered. He wrapped his fingers inside his wife's, and Father Time rekindled a connection he had only ever had with her. He surrendered to that sensation and felt the final drops of their lives touch one another, like water in a cave, top meets bottom, Heaven meets Earth.

As their eyes closed, a different set of eyes opened, and they rose from the ground as a shared soul, up and up, a sun and a moon in a single sky.

EPILOGUE

80

Sarah Lemon was rushed to the hospital.

She stayed there overnight. Her lungs cleared and her head stopped throbbing and she reminded herself how lucky she had been that her phone had rung with a loud, heavy-metal guitar riff—programmed by Ethan—which signaled her mother, calling to wish her a Happy New Year.

The noise had startled Sarah just enough to realize what was happening, and she pressed the garage opener and pulled the car door handle and fell out. She crawled along the concrete floor, coughing violently, until she reached the outside air. A neighbor spotted her sprawled in the snow and called 911.

She was admitted to the emergency room as the clock struck twelve and people up and down the coast screamed in celebration.

On the gurney next to Sarah was a man named Victor Delamonte.

He'd been admitted moments earlier, suffering from cancer and kidney disease. He apparently had been off his dialysis, which was addressed with a blood transfusion, although the man who brought him in said only that he'd been complaining of abdominal pain.

What was never revealed was how Victor altered his end-of-life plans. As he was lifted for immersion into ice, his eyes popped opened and he saw Roger. Victor had instructed Roger, in the whispered conversation earlier that evening, that if for some reason, any reason, he changed his mind about this idea, he would signal it by saying a single word, and Roger would abort the plan.

Do you understand? No hesitation if that happens?

I understand.

It happened. A word was spoken. Upon hearing it, Roger screamed, "Hold it right now!" He forced the coroner and doctor to back away, then immediately called for an ambulance. He followed his boss's orders, as he always did, because he'd listened for the word and the word was clear:

"Grace."

81

This is a story about the meaning of time,

and it begins long ago, but it ends years from now, in a crowded ballroom, where a respected research doctor is applauded by a crowd. She credits her colleagues. She calls it "a team effort." But the man who introduces her expresses the worldwide opinion that Dr. Sarah Lemon has found a cure for the most dreaded disease of our time; it will save millions of people, and life will never be the same.

"Take a bow," the man says.

She lowers her head. She waves meekly. She thanks her teachers and research partners and she introduces her mother, Lorraine, who stands, holding her handbag, and smiles. Sarah also notes that this would never have been possible if not for a benefactor named Victor Delamonte, who, back when she was applying to colleges, had generously bequeathed her entire tuition costs to an Ivy League university—undergraduate, medical school, as far as she could go—in his last will and testament, a document that was changed drastically just before he died from the very disease for which Sarah had now found a cure. He had survived only three months beyond their night together in the emergency room. But his wife, Grace, said those were the most precious months of their marriage.

"Thank you all very much," Sarah concludes.

The crowd rises in an ovation.

Meanwhile, at the same time, on a cobblestone street in lower Manhattan, a new tenant is moving into One Forty-Three

Orchard. A construction crew is knocking down walls, as per the blueprints.

"Whoa," one of them says.

"What?" says another.

Flashlights shine into a cavernous space, previously hidden below floor level. On the walls are carvings, every shape and symbol imaginable. In the corner is an hourglass, holding a single grain of sand.

And as that glass is lifted by curious workers, someplace far away—someplace indescribable in the pages of a book—a man named Dor and a woman named Alli run barefoot up a hillside, tossing stones, laughing with their children, and time never crosses their minds.

⊰ ACKNOWLEDGMENTS ⊱

First, thanks to God. I do nothing without His grace.

Some books are tougher than others. Thanks to all who showed patience with me on this one and who believed in the idea right from the start. My family, my siblings, my siblings-in-law, and my dear pals.

A special thanks to Rosey and Chad, who redefined the word "friend"; they filled the unforgiving days with endless support. I will never forget it. Also, a deep thanks to Ali, Rosey, Rick, and Tricia, who gave this book its first look and encouraged me that Father Time had a story to tell.

An unending thanks to Kerri, who not only read and copy-edited these pages, but fended off all disturbances, allowing the story to breathe and find its place in the world. And to Mendel, who is a bum, but who arrived in the office to save the day.

Thanks to David, for a quarter century of believing in me, and to Antonella, Susan, Allie, David L., and the rest of Team Black Inc., for being the raft in the ocean that they always are. Thanks to Ellen, Elisabeth, Samantha, Kristin, Jill, and all the gang at Hyperion, and to SallyAnne for publicity. And a deep thanks to my editor, Will Schwalbe, who said yes when we asked, and who made me happy that he did.

A special note of thanks to the Cryonics Institute in Clinton Township, Michigan, and the staff members who shared information freely for this novel. While Victor learns a certain lesson in these pages, no judgment is meant to be passed on the science of cryonics or the choices of its practitioners and patients. This is, after all, a fictional fable.

As with everything, a thanks to my mother, father, Cara, Peter, and all my extended family.

Finally, there is only one Alli in my life, and all that Dor saw in his, I see in mine every day. Thank you, Janine.

And to my faithful readers, the ones who picked up this book without even asking what it was about—you are the backbone of my work, and the eyes I have in mind when I type my sentences. May I continue to provide you a fraction of the hope and inspiration that you provide me.

Mitch Albom
Detroit, Michigan
May 2012